Lock Down Publications and Ca$h
Presents

I0666772

Hood
Consigliere 3
CAUSE AND EFFECT

Written By
KEESE

First Edition 2025

Printed in the United States of America

Lock Down Publications
P.O. Box 944
Stockbridge, GA 30281
www.lockdownpublications.com

Like our page on Facebook: Lock Down Publications
www.facebook.com/lockdownpublications.ldp

Stay Connected with Us!

Text **LOCKDOWN** to 22828 to stay up-to-date with new releases, sneak peaks, contests and more…

Like our page on Facebook:
Lock Down Publications

Join Lock Down Publications/The New Era Reading Group

Visit our website:
www.lockdownpublications.com

Follow us on Instagram:
Lock Down Publications

Email Us: We want to hear from you!

Chapter 1

Ten Years Later

"Hmm-hm-hmmm…" Sunami hummed along to a classic by Babyface, as he removed a pot from the oven.

Sunami had fried turkey bacon keeping warm in the microwave. Butter cheese grits were cooling on a pot coaster with fresh coffee brewing on a nearby counter. Sunami hit the off switch on the oven after noticing the wheat bread he had been toasting was done. "Almost ready!" Sunami murmured to himself, as he cracked open five eggs and began scrambling inside the skillet.

Meanwhile, upstairs in the master bedroom was Hypnotic, Sunami's wife. She was still asleep and completely unaware of the surprise she was about to welcome. Christmas was less than two weeks away. But for Hypnotic, her Christmas and birthday wishes (which had been the same for the past two years) were about to come true. She just didn't know it yet.

I can't wait to see the expression on her face when I tell her the news, Sunami thought to himself, as he toted the food upstairs on a breakfast in bed serving dish. Sunami had been a jack boy when he first met Hypnotic. The two had met at a gas station. Hypnotic had come along at the perfect time in Sunami's life. After collecting the large sum of Shadow's insurance policy, Sunami and Hypnotic moved into a condo in Manhattan, and Sunami and his cousin, York, linked together and opened numerous lucrative businesses. Hypnotic had come along and provided Sunami with the type of care and love he'd desperately needed, and unlike other diversified divas, Hypnotic's love wasn't motivated by greed or prestige. Her love was enthused by her spirt – a spirit that commanded her to love unconditionally. Hypnotic's unconditional love had been tested from the very beginning. She had vehemently objected to Sunami's business plans. The idea of opening and operating a moving company and real estate company was the plan Sunami had chosen; a plan Hypnotic initially had loved before Sunami revealed to her his true agenda. The companies would operate as advertised on the surface. But beneath the surface, the moving company would load and ship illegal goods and drugs. And the real estate properties would be used to store said products. Or it would operate as ghost shippers or receivers' addresses when needed. And this had been the reason for Hypnotic's stern objections – an opinion he still held two years later.

With Hypnotic, all the money, the cars, and the hoes didn't matter. The salons, detail shops, and bodegas mattered. Since the beginning, all Hypnotic had ever wanted was for Sunami to withdraw from any and all illegal enterprises. Sunami's schemes had, thus far, worked out beautifully. His moving company had expanded from one building and two eighteen-wheeler trucks to twelve buildings and sixty trucks, spread out globally strategically in New York and Connecticut with nine enterprises in New York alone. The real estate company had taken off from the very beginning. To date, it remained Sunami and York's greatest asset. Almost 3/4th of Sunami Wolfpack Inc.'s yearly assets came from real estate sales. Sunami and York were both multimillionaires. So, with his money made and his 38th birthday nearing, Sunami found himself compelled to finally give his wife her wish.

"Ummm… M… Um!" Sunami moaned with pleasure, as he admired how beautiful his wife looked as she slept.

But Hypnotic wasn't sleep. She was, as they say, playing possum. The aroma of the food as it was cooking had already awakened her. Hypnotic had even crept downstairs and spied on Sunami as he stood over the stove in chef mode. And while doing so, by utter luck, she noticed the breakfast tray. It didn't take Hypnotic long to put one and one together. So, with her heart fluttering with joyfulness, Hypnotic crept back into her bed to await her husband's arrival. But now, with him upon her, Hypnotic fought with all her might to keep Sunami from knowing she was playing possum. But as soon as he set the tray above her waist and whispered in her ear, Hypnotic burst into laughter.

"I can't believe this! How'd you know?" Sunami asked Hypnotic, as she centered herself beneath the tray.

God, I love this man, she thought, as she leaned forward and kissed Sunami passionately.

"Damn! I gotta do this more often," Sunami said after receiving Hypnotic's sensual kiss of gratitude.

"You'll get no objections from me," Hypnotic replied, as she lifted her coffee demitasse and blew in it.

"I bet my life you won't object to my next surprise either."

"Oh, how I love surprises," Hypnotic playfully noted.

"Well, as of the 19th of this month… I'm retiring from Wolfpack Inc."

"What!?! Are you serious?" Hypnotic asked, replacing her cup of coffee on the tray.

"Yeah, I'm serious. It makes no sense for me to stay in the game. We got more than enough money. Your salons and our detail shops and bodegas are doing well enough to sustain us. At least until we find our next worthwhile investment," Sunami answered, as he reached over and held his wife's hands.

"So, let me get this right. You severing all ties to Wolfpack Inc. and going one hundred percent *legit*?" Hypnotic asked apprehensively.

"Yes, Hypnotic! I'm relinquishing all rights to Wolfpack Inc. I'm going square, baby. I thought you'd be happy…" Sunami stated, as he watched Hypnotic lower her head and stare at her tray of food. "I thought this was what you wanted," Sunami added nervously, as he took the tips of his fingers and lifted Hypnotic's chin.

When Sunami looked into his wife's angelic eyes, he knew his surprise had been well received. Hypnotic's approval came not from her words but her tears. Tears which streamed abundantly from her eyes, from the depth of her soul, spoke profoundly to Sunami's heart. And at that moment, Sunami realized, all at once, just how selfish, lucky, and above all else how fortunate he'd truly been since their first encounter. Sunami quickly maneuvered around the tray and embraced his wife passionately.

"Thank you, baby… Thank… Oh, God, thank you!" Hypnotic sobbed out the words, as she cleaved tightly to her husband.

"No, baby! Thank you!" Sunami stated. He held his wife, as he silently and profusely thanked God for blessing him with the opportunity to share a moment such as this with his *forever* woman.

December 19
11:50 p.m. – 40/40 Club
The place was jumping. D.J. Khaled was behind the wheels and had Lil Baby resonating through the club. Everywhere a person looked, trap stars and celebrities — with their entourage or with the diversified diva they were pursuing — were popping bottles of Gold as if they were the drinks available. The room was full of aromas that were created when a multitude of various types of weed smoke were combined. It was this smoke that caused Sunami to choke and briefly cough, as he continued to scan the room. He noticed Lopez, one of his workers, over by a second bar with his pants strangely tight but sagging. He was pretending

to dance with some model chick he was really smashing. Shaking his head in disbelief, Sunami turned away from Lopez and caught sight of a number of his other workers partying like real rockstars.

"I know he not snoring dope off that girl's ass!" Hypnotic stated, as she wrapped her arms around Sunami's waist.

As he sought out the dope fiend in question, Sunami noticed York making his way toward him. But York wasn't alone. Following at his heels were six others. *Good! He right on time*, Sunami thought, as he motioned them over to the empty table and chairs at his rear. "Tell the waiter to bring over the drinks. I'll handle Khaled," Sunami stated, as he hoisted up the flashlight he'd been holding and began shining its beam of light directly into D.J. Khaled's face. This was already agreed upon as the cue that would stop the music. "Take a seat. This won't take long," Sunami said to his four top wolves and their lady loves.

"Just place the tray on the table," Hypnotic instructed the waiter, as he obeyed and deposited the tray full of gold bottles. The crowd was beginning to stir from the silence when Sunami grabbed a glass of champagne with his left hand and a wireless microphone in his right.

"What's going on?" Zahir, one of Sunami's top dogs, asked York, as he watched Sunami beckon for the crowd's attention.

"We about to find out together," York replied, as he took his glass of champagne from the tray. At the far end of the table sat Animal and his lady, Drea. Animal was another one of Sunami's top wolves. To hear him tell it, he was Sunami's number two man, behind only York, who served as Sunami's consigliere. Animal was beyond ambitious, and his lady, Drea, was even a worse demon. Drea's motives exceeded mere ambition and were shamelessly sinister. And for the advancement of her man's status, there were no limits to what she'd do. These qualities, when paired with the right street codes, made one hellava demonic woman, a true asset to any team, but with Drea, there was no code. If she could get away with killing York to seat her man next to Sunami in the line for power, she would. Drea's hunger didn't allow her to see the benefits of co-existing in a Teflon coated crime family. All she desired was the throne. And getting her man there was all she lived for. Drea had long ago reeled in Sunami's wife, Hypnotic. Drea created a wedge to estrange Hypnotic from the spouses of the other top wolves. By isolating Hypnotic, Drea became privy to knowledge that Hypnotic felt she couldn't trust the other ladies in the family with. That was how Drea knew what Sunami was about to announce. She had gotten the heads up from a jubilant Hypnotic, who couldn't wait to let her know that Sunami was going square.

Sunami's retirement from the game left only one logical order of ascension. York would take over, and Animal would become his consigliere.

If everything goes as planned, me and my man about to run New York, Drea thought to herself, as she rubbed the back of her man's neck to calm him. "Relax, baby, tonight you become consigliere," Drea whispered into Animal's ear, seeking to erase her man's nerves.

"It's about damn time!" Animal, in a half mumble, replied, as he watched the crowd of lower-level crew members, their ladies, or the call girls hired to entertain, formed rows around them, preparing for Sunami's speech. Sunami stood in front of the long, rectangular shaped table that was prepared for him and his top wolf.

Behind the table, to his left, sat York. And to York's left was the following: Zahir, Erin, Pam, Raquel, Drea, and at the end of the table sat Animal. York was still dazed from the private conversation he and Sunami had previously held that night. But Sunami's revelation to York wasn't the only reason for York's semi-befuddled mental state. York's answer to Sunami's official move left him just as baffled as his boss' announcement was bound to leave the crowd in attendance. *However. it is now time to drop the bomb*, Sunami thought, as he cleared his throat.

"I won't waste your time with some long, drawn-out speech. I'll keep this short and sweet. What you're about to hear is a finalized decision. Non debatable," Sunami said, as he looked to York and motioned for him to come stand next to him. "As of midnight tonight, I am no longer the head of this cartel. I'm retiring," Sunami proclaimed before the buzzing whisper of the crowd forced him to pause.

'They're taking the news better than I did," York whispered to Sunami, as he stopped to stand just left of his boss.

"As you all know, my successor, naturally, is York, my long acting, trusted consigliere. However, York has declined the offer to become family head." A multitude of astonished utterances erupted all through the club.

"What the fuck?!" Drea blurted out, as her eyes shot daggers at Hypnotic's back. Her response drew her and Animal the stares of all at the table. After once more calming down the crowd, Sunami continued.

"York must choose between Animal, Raquel, or Zahir to become the new head of this cartel. But until that choice is made, York is the head of this family. And with that said, I want everyone to raise they glass for the new boss... to York!" Sunami stated, as he, Hypnotic, and York clanged their champagne flutes to cap off the toast. The table behind the trio – and the crowd before them – were, no doubt, still very much shell shocked. But none dared outwardly show it. So, York, Sunami, Animal, Raquel, and Zahir sat at the table, discussing the finer details of what just took place.

"What do you mean remove your name from contention?" York asked, as Raquel rose from her chair.

"I don't care about the position. Consigliere?! Now that I would consider. But being boss?! Nah! I'm good. Just know that I support whoever you choose. My loyalty to you – or whomever you appoint as head – shall remain unwavering,"

Raquel stated, as she acknowledged all at the table with a nod of her head then departed.

"And then it was two," Animal said, as he glanced at Sunami and York smugly.

"York has informed me he needs more time to decide between you two. So, I'm giving him until Sunday morn to choose. He's assured me he would be ready with a decision by then," Sunami stated, as he told Animal and Zahir about the conclusion finally reached by him and York.

"Cool! Well, just let me know where to be and I'm there," Zahir stated, as he rose and shook Sunami's hand.

"Yeah! What he said?" Animal masterfully pretended like he didn't hear Zahir's response.

"Go enjoy the party. I need to speak with York a minute," Sunami stated.

Sunami continued to speak, as York watched Zahir and Animal mingle into the crowd. York was clueless to what Sunami was saying. HIs mind was focused on processing one thing and one thing only. *Who do I choose?*

Chapter 2

York's face was buried into his pillow. His body was completely drenched with sweat. His mind and body were at war. Both were fighting two different battles, however. Normally, York's wife would have noticed his distress. But not tonight. Tonight, Pam was too busy getting long dicked to notice. York had Pam's back pinned to the king-sized bed. Her hips were raised by three pillows, allowing York to obtain deeper penetration. Pam was a thick, chocolate sister. The coating of her skin was exactly the same shade as India Arie's; the queen who sang *Brown Skin* was coincidentally also streaming from the couple's in house stereo. Pam was a lot of woman – not overweight but a wonderfully curvaceous, voluptuous woman. Her desirable G cup breasts were pinned to her chest by York's chest. Her arms were wrapped around her man's shoulders, her fingers digging into the flesh of his upper back. York held her legs open wide with the folds of his arms while gripping her ass cheeks for additional leverage, as he savagely fed dick to her pussy.

"Ahh-ohh-oo-ahh!" Pam wailed, as she floated from one orgasm to another. Pam didn't get tired from her orgasms. Instead, each orgasm only fueled her fires more. Never had she achieved more than five orgasms with any of her past lovers. But tonight, York had shattered that previous climatic plateau. Pam was certain she'd had at least ten orgasms but had since lost count. All she could do was dig her nails into York's flesh and hang on for dear life, as York fucked her senseless. *Ohh-shit!* was the only coherent thought that continuously popped into Pam's mind as waves of sexual pleasure pushed her farther and farther over the edge. But York was clueless to the fact. York couldn't hear Pam's screams of pleasure nor was he aware of the large puddle of cum that lay beneath he and Pam.

York was relieving stress. And due to the importance of his decision, York was all the more driven to make the right choice.

Animal or Zahir? York thought, as he continued to hammer away at Pam's extremely wet pussy. For sheer intimidation purposes, Animal was the logical choice. As consigliere, it was York's job to cover the boss' shortcomings. This fact alone made the choice all the more hard. Animal could be difficult at times, but he could and would make a suitable boss. But Zahir was like family to York which made him the sentimental choice for him. But this was what bothered York the most. He hated to believe that people would think he would choose Zahir out of sheer favoritism. But the fact of the matter was, some would think just that.

"Ahh! Ohh-fuck!" York yelled out, as his seed finally erupted from his loins, coating the inner lining of the vaginal walls of his lady love. After receiving his seed, within seconds, Pam was floating off into an orgasmic slumber. York lay upon her, completely exhausted and fighting to catch his breath. After some time, he finally calmed his breathing, and in doing so, he also regained his peace. For it was in that moment that he made his decision.

In the morning, must... call... Sunami. Then... call... York thought, as sleep overpowered him before he could complete his thought.

***

Oh, hell no! York mentally screamed, as he was awakened out of his sleep by music blaring from the living room. Gazing over at Pam, York found her resting peacefully with a smile beaming across her face. She was deep asleep, completely unfazed by the ruckus stirring from the lying room, a ruckus that could only originate from one source.

"Ja-Ja!" York yelled, as he entered the living room, seeking to gain his daughter's attention. Ja-Ja was four years old and was a bundle of energy. In many ways, she was much like her dad – devious when she wanted to be, silly when she felt like it, and always learning something new. And this morning, Ja-Ja was being bluntly devious.

"Bout time!" Ja-Ja said, as she noticed her dad and immediately turned off the stereo.

"What you say?!" York asked, a bit shocked at the statement of his daughter.

"Hurry up! You get the cereal and milk. I'll get the bowls and spoons," Ja-Ja replied, totally ignoring her father's question, as she turned away from him and headed into the kitchen.

"Shit!" York half mumbled to himself, as he realized he had forgotten he promised to watch cartoons and eat cereal with Ja-Ja this weekend.

York's initial agitation began to fade, quickly replaced by a sense of pride. His daughter had schemed and orchestrated all the confusion needed to compel her dad to honor his promise. With a smirk adorning his face, York glanced at the T.V., a square piece of cornbread-looking character with pants, that the other toons called Bob, danced across the screen. At Ja-Ja's age, he had schemed much the way she had – except he hadn't been trying to watch cartoons. Oh, no! York's first scheme had damn near resulted in murder.

Ring-A-Ling-A-Ling!

His name was Bobby Goldstein. And for months, he had been snitching on York and his homie, Kenny. That day, payback would be theirs. York could feel all the old hate from that time re-stirring within him once again. *Damn, I hated that Jew!* York thought, as he resumed his flashback.

"They killed Cornbread!" That phrase from the movie, *Cornbread, Earl, and Me*, haunted York's early childhood. It gave him the wrong initial views of cops and white people as a whole. But while other kids were watching Bugs Bunny, York was watching *Roots*. And his adolescent hate became so strong that it eventually overwhelmed him. Bobby Goldstein was the proverbial straw that broke York's fragile resolve.

There was a reason why movies were given content ratings, as well a reason why kids shouldn't be prematurely exposed to such content. However, Bobby would find out the hard way what happened when one did.

"Ah-agh!" Bobby gurgled, as York took a broken piece of window blind string and choked him mercilessly.

It was arts and craft day for Ms. Simon's second grade class. And while she taught the students how to make piñatas, Lil York and his homie, Kenny, had baited Bobby's nosy ass into a shielded corner. Once they got Bobby behind the portable drawing board, he was completely at their mercy. When York first began his assault, Bobby had attempted to dash to the back door. But Kenny caught him with a mean two piece that sent Bobby staggering. Enraged at Bobby's attempt to flee, Lil York began to choke Bobby with all his might. Kenny covered the Jew boy's mouth, eliminating any chance for his cries for help to be heard. Bobby's face turned three shades of red, as the lack of air to the brain caused his body to go limp.

Bobby was about to see white lights of death when someone snatched York off of Bobby. "You fucking snitch!" York yelled at the slumped-out Bobby. As soon as Ms. Simon snatched him off of Bobby, she franticly tried to revive Bobby.

"Come on!" Kenny said, as he pulled York by his arm, snapping him out of his daze. The two dashed for the schools' basketball courts to escape the melee of their classroom.

"Damn, yo! You almost killed dude!" Kenny stated, as he grabbed a basketball and began to bounce it.

"Yo, that's my word. When I was choking dude, all I could think about was that Roots shit," York commented, as he ran after the air ball Kenny had just tossed up.

The ball rolled until a pair of black, shiny, patent leather shoes entrapped it. "I think we need to talk," one of the school's three security guards stated. With about ten yards between him and the guard, York turned to run. But when he turned, he saw the school's other guards carrying Kenny, who looked none too pleased.

"Now, let's not be difficult. Come! Let's talk," the first guard said, as he led York toward the school's detainment center.

Vreen! Vreen! Vreen!

"Da-Da!"

The combination of the phone ringing and Ja-Ja screaming broke York out of his trance. "Yo!" York blurted out, answering his daughter.

"Come on. You gotta get the cereal," Ja-Ja screamed from the kitchen.

York had begun to walk toward the ringing phone when it stopped.

Pam must have got it, York thought, as he spun back toward the kitchen. "Here I come, lil momma!" he said, as he walked toward the kitchen.

"Ja-Ja! Ja-Ja! Come here!" Pam yelled from their bedroom.

"Agh!!" Ja-Ja groaned, as she took off up the stairs to see what Pam wanted.

As York watched Ja-Ja run off, he bugged out on how much like him she really was. But it was when Ja-Ja slipped on one of the steps that York's past once again took over his brain… Yak and G-face. That was the name of two Far Rockaway thugs who were putting in work around that time. They were part of a crew called the Red-Light Bandits. And the two guys' stick-up game was off the chain.

York had moved to his pop's hood in Edgemere, and this was due to the Bobby situation. But as soon as his feet hit the bricks, York was on the grind. At only ten years old, York had punked out two local bullies and was known to peeps in his circle as a true wild child. This was largely due to his strong arm game.

Though young, York had taken to robbing the bag boys who worked at the local Shop Rite grocery store. Because of his heart, Yak and G-face had gotten York to join them on a couple of moves. They robbed stores, cars at the local beach, and even neighborhood hustlers. This last lick (robbing hustlers) was how a real balls nigga came to hear about York. His name was Kareem, and he needed York to run interference for him and his peeps. The lick was to rob Jasper's, a local numbers spot. If successful, $,6000 would be York's cut. For a twelve-year-old, that was a lot of cream. York was definitely down. Before he could blink good, Kareem and his man, Tony, had parked their whip two blocks up from Jasper's.

"You sure you can handle this?" Kareem asked York, as they all hopped out the car.

"Give me the lighter and them firecrackers. I got this!" York replied. Kareem passed over the items.

"Now remember…"

"I know; I know!" York cut Kareem off, as he walked away from them and around the side of Jasper's Place.

The plan was simple; Tony would mingle out front until York was able to enter a very small window to the rear of the building. Once inside, York had to light all five firecrackers and toss them randomly. Once they exploded, that would trigger Tony into action. York climbed the crates alongside Jasper's Place and was through the window with ease. With only his upper body in the window and his legs hanging out, York went to work. As he lit all five stems that protruded from the firecrackers, no one within the numbers' spot noticed him. The customers were getting their gamble on, while the enforcers watched the front door and the ever growing pot.

Damn, I hope this works! York thought, as he noticed the spot had three enforcers. Without another thought, York tossed the firecrackers and bolted out the window. Pop–pop-pop! Pop-pop! That was the cue.

Tony sprang into the entrance of Jasper's just as the spot enforcers turned their backs to the front door. The third bouncer caught Tony's move and dove on top of Jasper, acting as his shield. Tony had entered the spot with his 9mm in hand and wasted no time making his presence known. His first two shots went into the table that blocked the enforcer that shielded Jasper. "Cover me!" Kareem yelled when he made his entrance, guns blazing.

The gamblers all laid face down, cowering, while Kareem busied himself grabbing the loot.

"Ugh!"

"Agh! Fu-ck!" screamed the other two enforcers, as Tony's bullets found home within their flesh.

Kareem and Tony wore ski masks, which allowed them to be as bold as they wanted, without anyone being able to make them out.

"Fuck! You killed him!" Kareem shouted to Tony, as he stood over Jasper and his enforcer's blood covered bodies. As Kareem stepped back, Tony stepped over to see for himself.

"Shit! Yo! Bounce. I got you covered," Tony told Kareem, as he turned his back on Jasper and his dead guard. Bang! Bang! Bang! Tony shot into the wall of the room where the other two wounded enforcers were concealed behind the wall. No sooner than Kareem headed toward the door, Jasper, who had been playing possum, opened his eyes. Facing him was the back of Tony's frame. Jasper pulled his

.380 from his ankle holster and let loose into the back of Tony's frame. All four of Jasper's shots found their mark.

"Agh! Fuck! I'm hit1 Yo, I'm hit!" Tony squealed, as he stumbled toward the door.

Kareem had heard the return fire and had doubled back for his man. But before doing so, he had tossed the 'Pantry Pride' sack of money to York and told him to carry it. Tony fell right into Kareem's arms, as he reentered Jasper's.

"Come on, nigga! I gotcha!" Kareem said to Tony, as he locked one arm around Tony and fired off shots from his .357 with the other. "Come on, nigga!" Kareem yelled to York, as he ran as fast as he could with Tony. Jasper's shots had caught Tony in the thigh, ass, kidney, and lung. Tony was leaking all over.

"Yo, fam! Ya mans not looking too good," York said, as Kareem continued to struggle to make it to their car with Tony.

"What the... Nigga, we ain't got time to rest!" Kareem yelled at Tony, who broke free from Kareem's grasp.

"Go... Just go... son!" Tony said, as he drew his 9mm on Kareem, daring him to rebuff his order. "Go!" Tony yelled, as he crumbled between two cars and laid out flat.

"Fuck! Come on!" Kareem said to York, as they both made a mad dash to the car.

York and Kareem got away. Or at least York did. True to his word, Kareem gave York his cut, and the two parted ways. After a few days of splurging out, York took $3,000 of his remaining $4,900 dollars and gave it to his mom. He had moved back in with her after the lick with Kareem went down. He told his mom he'd found the loot in the side alley. Little did he know, this little white lie would even save his life. About two weeks after the lick with Kareem, word had spread through the surrounding areas about Jasper or more appropriately stated, Jasper's revenge. Word on the street was that everyone involved with the robbery was dead. All except one. And word was that the last robber still breathing *was a midget. But due to York's sudden extravagant ways, the buzz around town quickly shifted toward him.*

As York made his way to his crib one day, two guys were mingling around his door. From the way it looked, his mom was steamed.

"York! Come here, boy!" York's mom shouted to her son.

"What's up?!" York asked his mom.

"These men say that money you brought home the other day belongs to them. And that you didn't find it but helped two others steal it. Now, tell me where you got hat money?" York's mom asked him.

"Mom, I told ya. In the alley up the way, like going towards Edgemere. I changed the bag it was in. But that's all I did. That's my..." York tried to explain, but his mom cut him off.

"You heard my son. So, if you negros think you gone Willie Lynch him, you motherfuckers got another thing coming. York, go inside and grab my red Liz Claiborne shoe box. Hurry up," York's mom said, as she spazzed out on the two accusers, showing her true Black Panther pride.

York was back at the door with the box in no time.

"You boot licking, suck ass, dick riding bums. Here... Take that shit. And get the fuck away from my door," York's mom screamed, as she flung the box of cash at them and slammed her door in their face.

"Mom, why you give them our money?!" York asked, trying hard to play dumb.

"It was the money or you. And Lord knows I'll go through hell before I let someone hurt my baby," York's mom said, as she walked into the kitchen and started preparing dinner.

Hurt me? But I... Man, fuck this. Tomorrow, I'm gone take the last of my loot and cop a gun, York thought to himself, as the reality of his actions finally set in...

"Da-Da! Here, it's Uncle Sunami," Ja-Ja said, as she came downstairs and gave the phone to her father.

"What's good, Mr. Square?!" York said into the phone, drawing the laughs of his longtime friend.

"Nothing much, just calling to let you know the meeting spot is Ms. Ce-Ce's Place. I'll be there by four this evening," Sunami said to York.

"Good cause I got your successor picked out," York responded, as he grabbed a blunt from the 'Dutch Master' box that laid on the living room's center table

"Ho-ho-hold up! Don't tell me who. Just surprise me when we get to Ms. Ce-Ce's," Sunami stated, as York agreed and continued to bust open the cigar, preparing to fill it with weed.

The two made small talk a bit more until York's other line beeped, signaling someone was trying to get through. However, by the time York tried to trace the call back, the operator's recording informed him that the previous caller had phoned from a restricted line.

Hmph! Now, who in the hell would call me from a restricted line? thought York, as he took a deep pull on his blunt and pondered the matter further.

Chapter 3

"Fuck! Nobody picked up. He might be over there with York. Fuck! York probably making him boss right as we speak!" Animal stated with agitation, as he paced the steps of Rockefeller Center.

"Be easy, baby. Zahir will show. He probably got caught up in the morning rush," Drea responded to her man through her Nextel chirp.

The couple had been in a continuous mad scramble ever since Sunami's announced retirement. Nobody ever suspected that York wouldn't succeed Sunami as boss. With York declining to ascend to family head, tension instantly materialized amongst the various ranks. Everyone had begun speaking on or pursuing ways to get their preferred top wolf selected as boss. And with Raquel bowing out, the odds were in Zahir's favor. That was why Animal and Drea were now roaming around Rockefeller Center. The two were seeking to tilt the scales of fate more into their favor. The two had hatched together a plan to have Zahir taken out of commission. The plan wasn't to murder him but to leave him severely maimed, which consequently would lead to Animal becoming boss by default.

In New York, the month of December was always an overly bustling time of the year, especially around Rockefeller Center. And the mornings were no exception. The tourists and commuting locals filled the immediate and surrounding areas. Some were carrying bags from early morning shopping. Others were sauntering and gliding across the ice. While even more people sipped on warm brews and made small talk. But in the crowed center lurked three troublemakers, three young, dumb gunners Animal had hired to perform today's job. None of the three were older than eighteen. Animal had been hearing about the little three-man team and knew they were known for small time stick-ups and busting their guns. But what Animal didn't know at first was that the three hoods badly wanted to be part of the Wolfpack Cartel. They called themselves Hammer, Shell, and Bullet. Their names were meant to symbolize the process of firing a gun. Animal learned about the trio's desire to be down when he asked them about the price of pulling off a hit. So, with the promise of becoming part of his cartel as payment, the trio accepted the job.

Animal's eyes, unable to locate Zahir, settled upon his three gunners. They were focused on Drea, who served as the trap's bait. Any man she led to the bench to her left was to be set ablaze.

And so, for the past half hour, everyone anxiously waited for Zahir. Then, just like a desert mirage, he appeared.

"He's right behind you." Animal alerted Drea through his chirp, as he ducked out of view.

"That must be the mark," Hammer said to his two accomplices, as they watched Drea turn and greet a man.

"I thought I was here to meet Sunami?" Zahir questioned Drea once they had completed their initial greetings.

"And you are. I'm just here to make sure Animal's here to meet him too," Drea stated in a tone that indicated she hadn't believed her man was really meeting with him.

"Oh, hell! Drea, if you gonna cause a scene, let the three of us handle business first. Alright?!" Zahir commented as he followed Drea toward the left bench.

"Me cause a scene?! Never that! Here, have some coffee," Drea replied, as she offered Zahir the spare cup of coffee she carried.

As soon as the first sip was swallowed, all hell broke loose.

Blat-ta-tat-tat-tat!

The sounds of automatic gunfire consumed the air. Zahir spun to peep the scene to see if he was in any imminent danger. With his back to her and fearing that he would draw his gun too soon, Drea flung her scalding coffee at Zahir, as she screamed and dove face first into the ground. The coffee served its purpose, causing Zahir to drop his own coffee, as he screamed from being drenched by the scalding brew. With Zahir momentarily distracted, this allowed Bullet the time he needed to circle behind him.

With so many people scrambling for cover or running for safer grounds, Zahir once again took in the scene. Two men, in ski masks, were shooting it out with the plaza police patrolmen. No longer feeling targeted, Zahir turned to locate Drea but was caught in the gut by something far hotter than coffee. *Shit! I'm hit!* Zahir thought, as he pulled his .44 caliber from his shoulder holster. Zahir wasted no time finding and going toward Drea. She laid sprawled next to the bench they'd been near. As he reached to pull her up, another bullet tore through his flesh. This time, the bullet half spun Zahir, as it entered and exited just below his heart. *Fuck! Those niggas trying to split my wig,* thought Zahir, as he staggered backwards and franticly scanned around for his attacker.

The world moved in super slow motion, as Zahir processed all that was transpiring. *I've been set up. But by who?!* Zahir thought, as his eyes caught the sight of the cops gunning down one of the two gunners they'd been exchanging gunfire with. The second gunner soon joined the first, as his persistent resistance was subdued with lethal force. Zahir, still staggering backwards, began to slide as his feet came in contact with the ice rink. While scrambling and seeking to regain balance, Zahir, by sheer chance, spotted his attacker. The gunman was crouched behind the bench that

Drea laid sprawled in front of with his gun zeroed in on Zahir. Bullet never saw the .44 caliber Zahir aimed at him. But he heard it. Bullet's final shot went awry as Zahir's two shots found their mark within his chest. Bullet was dead before he hit the ground. The ice beneath Zahir's feet, mixed with the kick that came with firing a .44 caliber twice, sent him into a half pirouette. His knees buckled, as he lost the battle to regain his balance and fell down upon his knees. This all took place as Animal scrambled down the steps of Rockefeller Center, seeking to avoid detection. He had witnessed the death of all perceived loose ends. Now, Animal needed to escape Zahir's detection to make the hit completely successful. But when Zahir crumbled to his knees, he came to rest directly facing the steps of Rockefeller Center.

Once Animal reached the last step, he looked toward Zahir once more and found himself staring into the face of his target. "Animal?! Help... hel-p," Zahir pleaded, never noticing the silencer equipped 9mm Animal had down and aimed at him.

"Are you okay, dude?!" a stranger asked, as he stepped between the two men, unaware that he'd just stepped between a predator and his prey. With a silencer attached and chaos still abuzz, Animal continued pointing his 9mm at Zahir with no fear of being detected by the plaza police.

"Lay down on the ice. Aw, fuck! You're leaking all over the place! Police! Police!" the white stranger stated, as he laid Zahir on the ice.

"Is he alright?" Drea asked the white stranger, as she cuffed and concealed Zahir's gun.

"Shit!" Animal said, as Drea's sudden appearance blocked his only shooting angle.

"I don't know. He's losing a lot of blood," the stranger answered, as Drea looked up and was shocked to see Animal hovering nearby.

25

"Sir, I'm a doctor. Step back please," some Hindu looking woman said, as she began giving aid to Zahir.

Drea looked from the woman back to Zahir. His eyes were looking directly at her. Contempt was written all over his face, as he glanced up at Drea. *He knows*, Drea thought, as she looked away from Zahir, seeking to locate Animal. He was nowhere in sight. *Good...* she thought, happy that Animal was smart enough to flee the scene before police could question him. *Now, I gotta figure out how to silence you before you can talk*, Drea said to herself, as she looked back down at Zahir, who began to lose consciousness.

Chapter 4

Smooch!

"Good morning, baby," Pam greeted York after kissing his cheek.

"It's about time you got up. You got a nigga about to starve to death in this motherfucker," York replied then took another pull of his blunt.

"I love you too, nigga!" Pam stated, as she mushed the back of York's head and made her way into the kitchen.

"Whatever! If you love a nigga, feed a nigga!" York said before flinching as Pam's approaching shadow caught the corner of his eye.

"Don't flinch now, nigga," Pam stated. as she drew her hand to hit York but snatched the blunt from his hand instead.

"So, that's how it's goin down, huh?!" York said after failing to re-obtain his blunt.

"Yep!" Pam replied, as she smiled playfully at her man and took a long, slow pull of the blunt.

"Ooooo! She smoking your funny smelling stuff," Ja-Ja said to her dad, seeking to create a rise from him.

"If you gone house the blunt, the least you can do is start cooking. You ain't slow. You can cook and smoke," York replied, as he grabbed another blunt out the Dutch Masters box and got ready to open it.

"I ain't cooking shit! Not until you get back from the store, that is…"

"And why am I going to the store?" York asked, as he stopped attempting to open the blunt's wrapper and awaited Pam's response.

"I can't make pancakes or omelets without any eggs. And while you at it, get some more bread, milk, and butter. Oh, and hurry up! A nigga hungry!" Pam sassily said, causing her and Ja-Ja to erupt in laughter, as York shook his head and conceded defeat...

***

The bell above the entrance/exit door of the grocery store rang, as York entered. "Sali, my man! What's popping?" York greeted the Punjabi storekeeper, as he headed toward the store's coolers to grab a carton of eggs, the milk, and the butter.

"York! My main man, what it be, me nigga?" Sali replied, as he, as usual, failed at his attempt to sound cool.

As York made his way down the aisle toward the cooler, his eyes fell upon a sight that made him stop dead in his tracks. The door of the cooler was flung wide open and bent over, rummaging inside the cooler, was some lady with an ass like a Montana mule. Either York had made a noise unconsciously or the lady just felt like she was being watched. Whatever the reason, she rose out of the cooler and turned and looked York square in the face. Instantaneously, her mouth fell open, and her eyes grew bigger than silver dollars. York had no doubt that his mouth and eyes looked the same. "Khadijah!" York stated, as he quickly regained his compose and looked her over. Khadijah said nothing, as she watched York look up and down her body. Before he realized it, York had traveled off into another flashback.

York was fifteen the last time he'd fucked Khadijah – or more appropriately stated, the night he snatched away her virginity. York and his man, Life, were out at a bustling spot called Styles, trying to sell the dope Khadijah swore to York

28

she'd found while emptying the trash, when they were approached by her pops, Hasan, who'd told them to return his dope – but not before Hasan ordered York to stay away from his daughter.

"Yo, son! You slow or something? The nigga just told you to stay away from that bitch!" Life tried to reason with York, as he watched him use the payphone to call Khadijah.

"Khadijah! Don't baby me! Naw! Look, meet me at my man, Life's crib! I don't care what you gotta do! Just get your ass to the spot!" York barked to her then hung up the phone.

"York, you wanna die, son?! The nigga flashed his gun for a reason!" Life said, restating nothing new to York.

"Be easy, son! I got this. Just let me use your crib's basement for a minute," York stated, as he and Life headed toward Life's place.

When they arrived at Life's crib, Khadijah was already there. She looked incredible, as she leaned against the front door of Life's spot. Neither York nor Life greeted her, as they entered his crib, sporting their best mean mugs. York snatched Khadijah by the hand and led her through the house and down the steps to the home's basement.

"Damn it, York! What the hell is your problem?!" Khadijah snappishly asked after she snatched her hand from York's grip.

"My problem is your pops! The motherfucker stepped to me and my mans at Styles. All behind you and your goddamn lies!" York said, as he closed the basement door and walked up on Khadijah.

"Lies?! I ain't told no lie!" she replied, holding her ground, as York now stood nose to nose with her.

"Oh! So, you gone keep lying, huh!? That's cool," York said, as he took his hands and began to unbuckle his belt.

"I told you I ain't... What you doing, York?!" Khadijah asked, as she watched York undo his buckle.

"Because of you, me and Life got clowned at Styles. Then your pops tell me to leave you alone. And now, you up in my

face telling more lies. You-you just straight disrespectful, huh?!" York said, as he slowly pulled off his belt.

"York! You need to chill. For real, baby!" she said, as she watched York fold his belt in two. "Stop!"

Before York could respond, Khadijah took off for the basement door. Her notion was sound, but York's had been better.

Pop! Pop!

"Aww, shit! Baby, don't do this!" Khadijah pleaded after York popped her ass twice with his thick, leather belt. Khadijah was cornered. At her back was the locked door of the basement and to her front stood York.

Hell yeah! Just like I thought. Now for step two, York thought, as he lowered the belt. "Why'd you have to lie?" York screamed, as he flung the belt at her feet.

"Baby, I'm-I'm sorry. I was only trying to keep you from having to rob niggas," Khadijah said, still somewhat skittish.

"Well, because of your lies and shit, we gotta break up," York stated, as he crossed the room and sat on the lone couch that occupied the basement.

"What do you mean we gotta break up?" she asked, walking near the couch.

"Your dad said as long as you're a virgin, I better not be caught near you," York replied, as he hung his head low.

"Or what?! Did he threaten you?" she asked, as she sat next to York.

"Sorta. He flashed his gun on me and Life," York said, as he lifted his head from out of his hands, allowing the wet spots beneath his eyes to be noticed by Khadijah.

"Baby, what's wrong?"

"Tonight, if we don't have sex, we gone have to break up," York said, as he hung his head once more.

"Says who? All we gotta do is say we did. My dad won't know if I'm still a virgin or not."

"Yes, he will," York replied, as he rose and turned his back to Khadijah.

'How?!" she asked, clearly befuddled.

"They got tests doctors can do on you to prove if you're still a virgin or not."

"But he-he wouldn't..."

"Bottom line, if we don't have sex tonight, we gotta break up," York said, as he turned back around to face Khadijah.

York remembered looking Khadijah up and down that day, much the same way he just finished doing in the aisle of the store. That day, they were both teenagers, trying to handle an adverse situation. At least that was what York had caused her to believe. The threat of Khadijah's dad was real – all except the bit about 'as long as Khadijah was a virgin'. That part was added by York. Since the moment York grabbed Khadijah's hand and led her to the basement, he had been running game. Even now, as the spit under his eyes, which posed as tears, dried, York was wearing his best 'please say yes' look. As he waited for Khadijah to break under the pressure of his faked crisis, her eyes were transfixed on some unknown spot on the basement's wall. She was obviously contemplating her options, as York continued to look as pitiful as possible while plotting on how he would fuck her once she said yes. Khadijah wore some black and purple suede Pumas with powder purple footies to match. Her button up cotton blouse was the same color purple as her shoes, and her tube skirt that fit her hips and ass like skin was jet black. *Damn, she look tasty*, York thought, as he watched Khadijah's thighs open wider, exposing to him her purple panties.

"Let's do it," Khadijah said, looking at York with an expression that said, "What other choice do I have?"

Yes! It's time I show your ass what's up! York mentally stated, as he approached Khadijah.

Ten minutes later, they were both naked, lying on top of three thick comforters. It had taken tons of coaxing to relax

"Why you lie?! Huh?1" York angrily questioned Khadijah, as he continued ripping apart the walls of her virginal pussy.

"Oohh-h! Nooo!" Khadijah sobbed, as tears welled up in her eyes from the pain and humiliation of being violated.

York never heard her cries. He'd long ago muted out her wailing. *"Answer me, muthafucka!"* York screamed out each word, as he pinned Khadijah's feet to the floor, as he folded her in two. York jackhammered into her pussy with savage force, as he continued to yell and berate Khadijah. Khadijah, after freeing her left hand, tried to fend for herself.

Slap! Bap!

"Get off of me, nigga!" Khadijah yelled after twice slapping York with all the power she could muster.

"Oh, okay!" York said in a half-stunned tone, as he rose on his knees and withdrew his dick from her.

Khadijah, still somewhat weary, slowly backed away from York, but before she could escape his arm's reach, York snatched her by her right ankle.

"You really think shit's sweet!" York said, as he quickly turned her onto her stomach. York sprang on the back of Khadijah. With his left forearm, he pinned her breasts and chest to the floor, and with his right hand, he aimed his cock for her asshole. *"Ungh!"* York grunted, as her ass proved too tight to ram into.

"No! Nooo! York! Don't-Don't, baby!" Khadijah pleaded with renewed fervor. If York in her pussy was unbearable, there was no way she could take the pain of York in her ass.

"Oh! I'm your baby now!" York mocked, as he spat on her asshole three times. Tears shot to her eyes once more when she felt York's spittle between her butt cheeks.

Khadijah knew, at that moment, there was no sense in protesting further. She was fucked, and as a sign of defeat, Khadijah made her entire body go limp, as she bit her bottom lip and braced herself for the inevitable

"Ungh! Aww! Oh, yeah!" York groaned, as he strained then broke through, entering her asshole fully.

"Gga-gawd! Oh-h! God!" Khadijah cried before York pushed her face into the floor and fucked her asshole the same as he'd fucked her cunt.

York fucked her asshole viciously. And when he finally did cum, he did so all over her face and hair. But possibly the worst part of Khadijah's humiliation came when York re-entered her bleeding, sore coochie and pissed inside of it. After using her pussy as his toilet, York stood over her with a look of disgust and contempt. "Get your lying, trifling ass the fuck outta my face!" he said, as he spat once more, this time on her breast.

York never saw her leave. He turned his back on her, as he put on his clothes.

And until today at the store, she'd never crossed his path again "Hmph! Funny how small the world can sometimes be," York said to the grown version of Khadijah, who still stood, speechless.

At the coy statement, Khadijah regained her senses and crept past York without giving reply to his comment. For a split second, York considered possibly apologizing to Khadijah for his past actions. *Fuck no! That bitch got what she deserved,* York mentally concluded, as he opened the cooler to get the eggs.

Meanwhile, in a three-level plush house in White Plains, the phone was ringing. "Hello… Calm down, girl. What's wrong? What! Oh, my God! Is he gonna make it? Erin, calm down. We're on our way," Pam said before hanging up.

"What's wrong?" Ja-Ja asked, as Pam dialed up York.

"Go get dressed. I'll tell you when you finish," Pam stated, as she waited for York to answer his cell.

"Hey, hey, hey!" York said, as he answered his celly.

"Baby, get home now! Zahir been shot… shot bad."

"What! Who?! I'm-I'm on my way," York replied then hung up his cell, as he dashed toward his whip.

Chapter 5

Mt. Sinai Hospital: noon.

"Booo hooo!" Erin cried uncontrollably for her critically injured lover.

Hypnotic and Drea tried to console her to no avail.

"Where the fuck is York at?" Raquel asked Sunami, as the two looked out the ICU waiting room window, searching for him.

"Speak of the devil," Sunami replied, as York and Pam made their way toward the waiting room.

"Now, Erin, you gotta calm down. You gotta stay strong for Zahir," Pam stated, as she entered before York and crossed the waiting room to help soothe Erin.

"What happened?" York asked, as he joined Raquel and Sunami by the window of the waiting room.

"Drea said some niggas went Kamikaze all over Rockefeller Center this morning. She say they weren't after Zahir. That he just got caught in the crossfire," Sunami answered with a tone that indicated to York that he wasn't at peace with Drea's story.

"You don't seem to be buying that though?" York framed the statement into a question.

"York, you know as well as I do that Zahir is too on point to get shot twice by random gunfire. One, I can see. But two! Naw, son! Something ain't right with that story," Sunami stated, as he looked York square in the eyes.

35

"You think someone put a hit out on Zahir?" York asked, looking from Sunami to Raquel.

"That's the only thing that makes sense," Sunami answered. "I just can't figure out who would have the heart to pull it off,' Sunami added, as he shook his head in disbelief.

"Rockefeller Center! Whoever they are, they got balls," Raquel added her two cents.

"So, how's Zahir?"

"The doc says he lost a lot of blood, and the bullet in his chest severed one of his heart arteries. He's in surgery as we speak," Raquel answered York, as her eyes filled with contempt.

"Oh, hell! Don't start, Raquel," Sunami stated, as he stepped in front of Raquel, blocking the view of the source of her scorn.

"What's wrong?" York questioned.

"Why the fuck she here? She ain't fooling nobody. Everyone know that bitch don't care for no one but herself," Raquel commented, as she turned to look back out the room's window. "Or him!" she added, as Animal approached the room.

"Yo, sorry I'm late. I came as soon as I heard," Animal stated, as he entered the room.

"Where you been?" York asked tersely. But before Animal could reply, his shadow interrupted.

"Hey, baby! Come here. You alright?" Drea said, as he slid into her arms for comfort.

"As I was saying, how's Zahir?' Animal asked, never answering the question posed by York.

"He's in surgery," Sunami answered.

"So, you gone ignore my question?" York said, his voice growing edgy.

"York, be easy," Sunami said, seeking to defuse a delicate matter.

"Sunami, no disrespect, but now that you've retired, that makes me boss," York said, as he walked up on Animal and Drea.

"York, I meant no disrespect. Me and Drea were going through some things last night. I spent the night at a hotel to give us some time to cool off," Animal stated before the tension grew any thicker.

The answer didn't sit well with York. But maybe that had to do with the uneasiness everyone felt and Zahir's ambush. "My bad, fam. I'm tripping," York said, then he turned to look at Sunami and Raquel. "We still on for five?" York asked Sunami, referring to their appointment to meet at Ms. Ce-Ce's Place.

"That depends on you."

"If you can change the time to ten o'clock, I should be good," York stated.

"Ten it is. What's up, York?!" Sunami asked, as he pulled York off to the side.

Once the two were out the hearing range of the others, York put it all on the table. "I need you to give me some time to hit the streets. A move this wild don't go down without someone knowing something."

"So, what's the plan?" Sunami asked.

"I need you to leave with your wife. Make sure y'all take Drea with you."

"York, what's up? Why you got me and Hypnotic playing escort to Drea?" Sunami questioned.

"I'm leaving Raquel to watch over Zahir. I trust she'll keep him safe. I'll get my lady to stay with Erin to keep her company. But with me and you gone, no one will be here to keep Raquel off Drea's ass."

"Animal. He'll keep them apart," Sunami suggested.

"Nah! He'll be with me," York replied, as his plan finally sunk into Sunami.

"I gotcha. If you need anything, call me. Alright?" Sunami said then headed toward the ladies after York agreed to notify him if needed.

York wasted no time dispensing his orders. "Raquel, call Mag and tell him to come help you watch the door. Me and Animal gone see what we can find out. Call me when you hear more about Zahir," York stated then turned and re-approached Animal. "I need you to come with me. We got some doors that need to be kicked in."

"Alright," Animal stated, as he drew away from Drea and followed York out the waiting room.

"Excuse me, sir. Can you tell me how the surgery is going?" York asked the surgeon that had just exited the operation room that housed Zahir. The man looked somewhat befuddled, and he pondered over how to answer York. The surgeon's anxiety-fueled hesitation was easily detected. "What the hell is going on?" York contemplated, as his eyes roamed over the surgeon's smock — a smock stained with blood. York's nostrils flared, and his blood began to boil, as he began to recall the only time he'd been shot...

"Butchee and the spot, boys. That's when it happened." York remembered, as he recollected the details of that day. York had been the block supplier for Butchee back then. Whenever one of Butchee's spots went dry, York was deployed to pick up the loot and re-supply the worker with a fresh package. It was on one of these occasions that York first found out just how hot a gunshot could be. York had just exited the elevator on the third floor when his instincts went haywire.

Something's not right, York thought, as he paused mid-step and began to scan the scene. Everywhere he looked, he found cause for concern. The door to the spot he was headed for was wide open. That wasn't right. Two guys ahead of York, but past the door, were moving strangely. But with their backs to York, both immensely focused on the hall's corner, York dismissed the notion as nothing more than paranoia. As York looked away from them and over his shoulder, he noticed a guy five or so steps away. He looked away from York when their eyes met and pulled on his cigarette again, as York exhaled the breath he'd been unconsciously holding. I'm tripping, York mentally concluded, as he turned back toward the door. Before his head could completely face the door, York noticed a sudden moving, causing him to flinch and turn his view back toward his rear. But while starting to do this, a form popped out the door, starling York enough to reach for his piece.

"Yo, York! I wouldn't do that," the form in the door said, as he held a .357 directly at York.

"Hand over the package," the man to York's rear said, as he began to close the gap between them.

In the time it took to blink, York went through his options. They want the work... They not gone let me live. Shit! Fuck it! York thought, then concluded, as he let his hand reach for the solution to his current problems.

"Oh, shit!" the man to Yorks' rear yelped out, as York spun and then shot him with his .38 Special. "Aww! Shit!" the man yelled, as he dove to the floor, trying to escape York's next shot. But York wasn't trying to shoot him anymore. His only goal was to get down the nearby stairs and out the guy in the doorway's line of fire.

Boom-boom-boom!

"Aww! Fuck!" York screamed, as two of the three shots fired found homes within his flesh. York never reached the stairs, as something tripped him up, causing him to slide on his back and lay sprawled out in front of the elevator. York tried to get back to his feet, but his body wouldn't listen to his mind's commands.

Fuck! Where the hell is my nigga, Life? York wondered to himself, as reality began to spin around him. Suddenly, York's eyes felt like they were being pulled by two ton weights. Though he tried, he was unable to keep them open. Though his eyes were closed, he remained conscious for the most part. As soon as his eyes shut, he felt someone tugging and snatching at him. To York's right, someone was moaning in pain. York tried with all his might to re-open his eyes, but his body continued to refuse. The painful waling of the guy York shot began to grow more faint, as York's attackers made their escape. After a brief moment of complete silence, the hallway erupted with the sound of curious onlookers.

"Oh, shit! York! York, can you hear me?" a female voice yelled at York from above, as he managed to find the reserve power needed to open his eyes. When his eyes did open, everything was blurry. It took him a few seconds to get his eyes to focus. But when they did, he noticed Crystal standing above him.

"York! Can you understand me?! Say something!" Crystal yelled down to York. She knelt down to get close to York and raised her hand to slap him.

"Cry-Crystal..." York uttered as fast as he could, seeking to avoid being slapped. "Take this... Call for help," York said to Crystal, as he handed her his gun.

As soon as Crystal tucked the gun, she rose to her feet and peeled ass up the steps to call for help. Apparently, she had been successful because York woke up in a Peninsula Hospital bed with tubes, IVs, and staples — all painfully doing their part to heal him and hold him together.

"Fuck!" York groaned, as his entire body felt like it had been trampled upon by a herd of elephants. It didn't take long for reality to settle in, which was immediately accompanied by extreme paranoia. I got banged out. Who set me up? Are they still after me? The questions came in rapid succession, as York mentally grilled himself, each question holstering his paranoia even more. York had worked himself up so bad that every little sound he heard set his nerves more and more on edge. After reaching his wit's end, York called for a cab and

stood looking out the window of his room, but the pain was too much for him to handle.

Thud!

"Oww! Augh!" York moaned, as he fell and painfully crashed on top of the concrete canopy. Pain consumed York. Even the act of breathing was painful.

Beep! Beep!

The cab honked, growing impatient. York didn't want to move but knew the cab wouldn't wait forever. So, he dug down deep and found the strength to crawl to the edge of the canopy. Once there, York saw the cab's trunk was directly beneath him.

"Gotta... catch... ca..." York stated to himself, as he rolled on the canopy and landed upon the trunk of the cab.

"What the fuck?!" the African cabbie swore, as he hopped out his cab to see what had just crashed against his trunk. "Holy shit! What the fuck!" the cabbie swore, as his eyes took in the sight of the agony consuming York.

"Ta-take me... t-to Ha-Ham-Hamel's..." York ranted then passed out.

'Hey! Hey, you! Wakey the hell up!" the cabbie screamed at York, as he nudged him, trying to wake him.

Second floor room. His hospital room was directly above the concrete canopy that marked the hospital's emergency entrance. York's plan was simple. The cab would pull up at the entrance, and he would lower himself out the window and to the ground. Once he got into the cab, he'd head for his hood.

"Yeah, that's it. Just a little closer... That's it... Now park good.!" York ranted to himself, as he watched the cab he called park at the emergency entrance.

With nothing but a hospital gown on and metal stitches keeping him together, York opened his room's window to leave. But for the second time that day, York's body refused to follow orders. Whether lifting his arms, legs, or simply bending to lean out the window, York's every movement resulted in pain. But with possible death as a motivator, York managed to climb onto the window's outside ledge. Mind over matter, York thought to himself, as he sought to push his pain from the front of his mind. York gripped the windowsill with his hands and began lowering himself down onto the concrete canopy. But gravity pulling at his legs and the bite of the steel stitches as they dug into his stretching flesh proved to be too painful a duo.

"Yo, Crystal! Go check out that cab. It's been sitting on that corner for a minute," Life said, as he ducked into the shadows of the stoop and watched Crystal head for the cab.

Since York got clapped, everyone had been on edge. No one was taking any chances that weren't necessary.

"Yo, who you waiting on?" Crystal yelled to the cabbie through his passenger side window. Her sudden appearance startled the cabbie enough to reveal to Crystal what he had been smacking on.

"Huh! What?" York mumbled, as he came back to reality.

Oh, my God! York! Yo, Life! Come here. Hurry!" Crystal shouted, beckoning him over.

"Look, somebody need to pay me," the cabbie stated, as Life drew near.

"Yo, what's up?" Life asked, as he peeped into the cab.

"I need me money. That's what's up," the cabbie answered, as Crystal pointed to the half-conscious and moaning York in the cab's backseat.

"Oh, shit! York!"

"Are you deaf?! I need my money," the cabbie reiterated in response to Life's shocked outburst.

"Oh, you'll get your money alright. But first, you got some more work to do," Life replied, as he reached within his coat.

Chapter 6

Oh, shit! I'm gonna die, York thought, as he bolted as far as he could from the hospital bed. Pain gripped him instantly, causing him to slump back to the bed, as he yelped out from moving his body too quickly.

"York! Are you okay?!" Crystal asked from her seat next to his bed.

"Cry-Crystal! I must be... dreaming."

"Nope. Not a dream. I'm here, baby," Crystal stated, as she rose from her chair and began rubbing his chest.

"Can't stay... here. Gotta go..."

"Shhh! You gotta get some rest," Crystal soothingly commented, as she slid her left hand under York's cover and gown. York's breath caught in his throat, as he felt Crystal's hand wrap around his dick.

"Wha-What you doing?"

"Making sure you relaxed," Crystal answered York then dove headfirst, taking all of York's dick into her mouth.

"Umm!" York groaned, as his body tensed momentarily then relaxed, as Crystal went to work tongue fucking his dick.

Crystal was known all around southside Jamaica Queens for giving out the second-best blow jobs in all of New York, second only to "Wet Pussy". But she sucked York's cock like her life depended on it. And as he tensed then exploded, plastering her throat with his creamy cum, he released

43

completely. With a smile on his face, York drifted off into another world.

"Sir?! Sir, did you hear me?"

"Huh?!" York replied, as the doctor's voice startled him out of his flashback.

"I said the internal bleeding is causing some problems. But once we get that under control, we can proceed with our scheduled surgeries. Look, I need to get back inside. I'll have a nurse keep you posted," the doctor stated then walked off, leaving York and Animal looking dumbfounded and at a loss of words.

"Yo, York! You alright?!" Animal asked a bit nervously.

"Let's go," York stated, ignoring the question, as he led Animal toward the hospital's elevators.

Vreen-Vreen!

York and Animal had just opened the doors to York's tar black Range Rover when his celly rang. *Bout time*, York thought, as he checked the caller I.D. and noticed it was his man, Daytona! "Hold on... Yo, Animal! See what he knows," York ordered, as he flung the phone at Animal. York had called Daytona immediately after hearing the news about Zahir. Daytona was the hood version of Wendy Williams. While Wendy dished dirt on Black stars, Daytona knew everything about anyone worthwhile in any borough. York had long ago put Daytona on the cartel's payroll and considered the monthly payments as money well spent. Daytona had come through in the clutch many a time before. And as York bent toward the rear seat floormats, he couldn't help but be amazed at how fast Daytona had tracked the source of Zahir's attack.

Now, just a few inches away sat Animal. And as Animal caught the tossed celly and sat in the front passenger seat, his heart began pounding viciously. *Fuck! I wasn't prepared for this... I gotta find a way to buy me some time*, Animal thought to himself, as he spoke into the cell and gathered the info Daytona relayed.

Meanwhile, York was unlocking a hidden compartment placed under the rear floormats' carpeting. The compartment held a small arsenal of weapons. York pulled out a shoulder holster and a .44 caliber revolver and began strapping up. "You strapped?" York asked Animal as he hung up the celly.

"Yeah! I got niña," Animal replied, using slang to describe his 9mm.

"Alright! So, what Daytona say he found?" York asked, as he climbed behind the wheel of the Range Rover.

"He say the word on the street is that Chase is responsible. He out of Redfern but has connections to the 40's hood too," Animal replied, altering the named hoods Daytona had given.

"Hmph!" York stated, as he cranked the Range Rover.

"Daytona said he would call back once he had more info," Animal answered, hoping York would take his word, allowing him the time he needed to tie up his loose ends.

"Hmph! I guess that means we're heading to Redfern," York replied, throwing the Range Rover into gear and pulling off.

Phew! Okay, I bought me some time. Now, I gotta figure out how to keep York off track and still stay one step ahead of him, Animal thought to himself, as momentary relief was replaced by renewed tensions.

It took York and Animal no time to reach Redfern. But since their arrival, they'd spent the past twenty or so minutes watching one particular stoop for some guy named Chase.

Vreen-Vreen!

"What up?!" Animal stated, as he answered his phone.

"Daytona?" York silently mouthed out the name to Animal, who replied by holding up one finger to tell York to hold on.

Movement on the stoop that was under watch drew York's eyes back to the block. What he saw was a white crackhead wobbling and swaying down the stoop's steps. The sight wasn't out of the ordinary. But to York, the sight caused him to half smirk as he recalled a time when he'd been both happy and relieved to see a stumbling, white crackhead. York had been in his late teens when he'd found himself in a real tight spot. York had been gambling at the weed spot when he'd lost not some but all his cash. And with no money and a promise to keep to his lady, York had to find some fetti and fast.

"Yo, youngblood, you a'right?" Nanfu, the spot controller, asked, as he watched York roam the hallway of his spot's entrance restlessly.

"I need some loot, Nanfu. I promised my girl we was going out tonight. And that's my word. I'm not breaking my promise, yo!" York replied, as he pulled out his .38 Special and checked to see if it was loaded.

"Hold up, youngblood. You and I always been cool. Now don't go making my spot all hot, shooting and scaring off my clientele," Nanfu spoke, as he put his hand on his own piece just to be safe.

"Come on, Nanfu. You know me better than..."

"Yo, I need the hookup. One of you gots to know where I can score some coke," a quirky looking white guy stated as he rushed through the entrance of Nanfu's weed house.

"He's not your clientele," York commented, as he swung his gun hand behind his back and approached the white guy. Nanfu only shook his head and backed away, knowing shit was about to get real ugly. Real fast. "You looking for powder or that hard?" York asked the man as a means to get near the white guy without raising his suspicions.

"Fuck powder. I want that hard."

Bap! Bap! Bap!

"That hard enough?" York asked, as he took the butt of his .38 Special and pistol whipped the white fiend.

"Dude... Aug! Ugh! St-Stop! Augh!" the white fiend yelped and pleaded, as York pounded his skull with a barrage of blows.

The fiend, in his rush to run and flee York's attack, tripped over his own feet, falling face first on the floor. York was on him like five starving Somalians scraping over a chicken leg. York caught the fiend with two solid, sharp blows to the back of his dome. The second of which caused the fiend to pass out, as blood leaked from his face.

"All that yelling. Sounding like a little bitch," York stated, as he flipped the fiend on his back and began to rob him. As soon as York's hand touched the fiend's money grip, the fiend sat straight up and looked directly at York with an expression on his face that said, "Oh, hell naw!" The fiend's sudden resurrection startled York but not enough to scare him. York snatched his hand out the fiend's pocket, taking his money in the process. But before he could put any distance between himself and the fiend, the crackhead grabbed a firm hold of York's shirt and wouldn't let go.

"No! Noo!" the fiend yelled, as he tried to pull York nearer to him.

Damn, this fiend is strong, York thought, as he pocketed the dough and redrew his .38 to administer another pistol whipping upon the fiend. But before he could proceed, Nanfu came out of nowhere and mule kicked the shit out of the fiend. The kick was so sudden and vicious that the fiend let go of York's shirt, as he simultaneously slid across the floor, stopping only inches from the entrance. Dazed and confused, the fiend flailed around on the floor, seeking to regain his equilibrium.

"Go on, York! Get outta here!" Nanfu stated, as he helped a semi-bewildered York get back to his feet.

York wasted no time, as he beelined for the door. As soon as York's feet touched the front stoop, he realized he'd just jumped out the pan and into the fire. "Yo, shorty! What's up?!" York inquired, as he caught a small-time dope peddler in mid sprint.

"About two blocks back, them boys in blue pulling jump outs. Yo, you definitely better get low," the peddler said, as his eyes focused on York's shirt before he took back off.

Glancing at his shirt, York noticed why the young peddler had stared at him after giving him the head's up. York's velour top was covered with big blotches of blood, some of it still wet. Fuck! York thought, as he scrambled off the stoop and ran into a nearby crowd of ladies. The females were about seven deep, all standing around or sitting on a nearby bench. York ran up on the crew, seeking temporary cover. But instead, he ended up receiving a blessing in disguise. "Yo, shorties, show a brotha some love. I need y'all to..."

"York! Boy, what happened? Why you all covered in blood? Never mind. Here!" Stephanie said, as she tossed York a leather bomber she'd been wearing as she waited for him to show up for their date.

As soon as the coat was pulled on and York scanned the Ave., he saw squad lights less than a block away. "As soon as these cops leave, I'm gone... Fuck!"

"Fuck who?! Who you think you talking to?!" Stephanie began to spazz, feeling like York had disrespected her.

"Chill, love. Not like... shit!" York cursed again, as Stephanie and the other girls' eyes all followed York's. With the cops coasting through at a snail's pace, the white fiend made his way onto the stoop, soaked from head to waist in his own blood. The fiend stumbled and fell before he could reach the stoop's first step. Damn! I swear I don't need this shit! York thought, as he prayed for some divine intervention.

Before the fiend could regain his footing, Nanfu popped out the front door and yoked the fiend by the back of his collar, snatching him back into the weed spot – and not a minute too soon. As soon as the door to the weed spot closed, the cops' cruiser coasted by.

"Yo, York! Come on, let's go! That's him," Animal stated, as he pointed toward a pecan tan dude walking up the Ave. toward the stoop the two had been staking out.

The guy they'd been staking out the Ave. for was named Chase. And from the looks of Chase's body language, he appeared to be acting extremely noid.

Once the two found the place described, they flanked both sides of the door. "If he break fool, bang him out," York stated then with a motion of his head signaled for Animal to knock on the door.

Bam-Bam-Bam-Bam!

"Yo, Chase! Yo, Chase! Open up, son! I know you in there!" Animal yelled in between knocks.

Bam-Bam!

"Nigga, you done lost your mind?! Don't be banging on my..."

"Bitch, shut the fuck up! Tell Chase to step outside!" Animal yelled out, interrupting the lady screaming from behind the half-opened door. Animal's tone of voice and word usage caused the woman behind the partly opened door to gape open her mouth at him in dismay.

"Un un!" the chick stated, as she slammed the door back shut, catching the tip of Animal's left hand as she did.

"Aww! Shit! You bitch!" Animal yelped in pain, as the sound of a deadbolt being locked signified the lady behind the door was through talking.

"Shoot the looks," York ordered Animal, as he moved away from the threshold of the door to stand next to Animal.

Bang-Bang-Bang!

Animal's gunshots were immediately followed by the sounds of the woman screaming and York's kick that broke down the apartment door.

"Oh, God! Don't kill m-me," the chick pleaded, as she huddled under the living room table, seeking cover.

"Don't call for God now!" Animal screamed, as he snatched the woman from under the table and placed the barrel of his. 9 milli on her chest.

"Animal, move!" York ordered, as he watched Animal draw back his gun and back away. York stepped over and knelt beside the woman. She appeared to be a mixture of half black and Puerto Rican or something damn close. Even though she was in hysterics, she still looked very nice. All this passed through York's mind, as he took his .44 caliber and gently outlined her body with its barrel.

"I only ask a question once. If you lie to me or piss me off in any way… you'll die. Do you understand?" York stated, as he placed the barrel of his gun under her chin.

"Y-yes!" she replied.

"What's your name?" York asked.

"Rita."

"Rita. That's nice… Can you tell me where I can find Chase?" York calmly asked her.

"Downstairs… making sales," Rita answered, as tears and sobs overtook her.

"Shh! Don't cry. You're doing fine. Now, tell me, Rita, if Chase was on the run, where would he go?" York asked, as he signaled for Animal to check the rest of the apartment.

"I don't know… I-I've only known him a couple of months," Rita replied, as fresh sobs wracked her body.

"Hmm! Not what I wanted to hear," York commented, as he cocked back the hammer on his .44 caliber once more.

"I-I-don't know! I swear… I'm s-sorry," Rita pleaded for York to believe her.

"Nothing. He's not here," Animal stated, as he re-entered the living room.

York wasn't sure if he could believe Rita or not. But giving her the benefit of doubt, York turned and gave Animal a peculiar look.

"What?!" Animal asked York, thrown off by the gaze York threw his way.

"When looking for Chase, did yo come across a lot of men clothes or a few bits here and there?" York asked Animal, as he cut his eyes back at Rita.

"Not many… Why? What's up?" Animal replied.

"Nothing. Let's go…" York stated, as he reset the hammer of his .44 and stood to leave.

"What about the bitch?" Animal asked, as he moved near the apartment's entrance.

"Rita! Here! This should cover the door… And this… this should cover the funeral," York stated, as he peeled of two hundred at first then peeled off four thousand more and tossed them onto Rita's chest before turning to leave.

"Yo, York! Are you tripping?!" Animal stated, as he moved from the door toward where Rita lay.

"I'm leaving our friend, Chase, a message. I want him to know that when we meet, I'm bring death with me," York said, as he spun Animal back toward the crib's entrance and escorted him out.

Damn! I've never seen York break fool like this, Animal said to himself, as the sound of Rita's sobs grew faint, and his anxieties grew stronger.

"Who you know around this way that can help us find this nigga?" York asked Animal, as the two hopped back into the Range Rover.

"There's a freak named Kiyanna I know. She stay over by Shorefront Parkway. She might know something," Animal suggested, not trying to be helpful but more so to keep from re-calling Daytona.

With minimal traffic, it didn't take long for them to reach their destination. "Dayton Towers!" York exclaimed, as he looked upon the building they'd stopped in front of.

"What?! Is there something I need to know?" Animal asked, as he gripped the car's door handle.

With a smirk on his face, York shook his head and turned to look back out the driver's side window.

"Give me a few minutes. If she does know anything, she won't say if I'm with you. I won't be long," Animal stated then jumped out the Range and sprinted inside the building. In his haste to enter the building, Animal knocked over the janitor.

"Muthafucker, watch where you going!" the janitor cursed, as he picked himself up off the floor.

"Hmph! They still wearing Dickies," York said to himself, as he recalled the last time he was at Dayton Towers…

"You're sure this gone work?" York asked Nanfu, as the two waved and walked past the building security.

"Trust me, youngblood. Ain't no lick sweeter," Nanfu replied, as he put on his plastic gloves and threw York a pair so that he could do the same.

"Now stick to the plan and everything should go fine," Nanfu added, as he handed York a mop bucket.

The plan was easy enough. Mop the hall and wait for someone to stroll by worth robbing. Once a target was found, York would signal for Nanfu by causing a distraction, and since they were on the top floor. they had no worries about security crashing the set. York mopped near the stairs, allowing him to maintain a constant eye on any movement in the hall.

Bingo! York said to himself, as he watched a couple and their child exit their pad.

Nanfu had only taken five or so steps away from York when he heard the sound of the mop's handle hitting the floor.

"Fuck! Fuck! Fuck!" York yelled, pretending to be frustrated.

"Excuse me, sir, but your language is very inappropriate," the father stated, as he walked toward York.

"Huh?!" York said, pretending to be confused, so Nanfu could get closer to the man's wife and kid.

"I said your lang…"

"Ohh! Shit!" shrilled the wife, as Nanfu put his .357 to her chest and covered her mouth to muffle the screams.

"What the hell?!" the father yelped, as he turned to check on his family and was pistol whipped from behind.

"Shut the fuck up. Open the crib or meet Jesus. Your choice," York told the white man, as he dug the barrel of his

.38 Special into the back of his skull. The man wasted no time opening up the door to his home. Nanfu, on cue, escorted the family into the home and proceeded to escort them to a room that had to be the little girl's. Once inside the room, Nanfu made the entire family get on their knees.

"If they move, shoot 'em," Nanfu stated to York then dashed out the room. Within a few minutes, Nanfu returned to the room with two pillowcases and a handful of broken electrical cords. "Bitch, get up! Here, tie up your family. Tie them up tight. If I feel too much slack, your husband gone taste some steel. Understand?" Nanfu said, as he tossed the stuff at her.

The items fell to the ground, and the woman dove headfirst toward the floor to retrieve them.

"Yo, take off that motherfucking mink, bitch," York said, as the chick got ready to grab the pillowcases and froze.

"You heard 'em, bitch. Take it off. And from now on, if you wanna live, you better do exactly what we say," Nanfu added

"Just think about slavery but reversed... Damn!" York added, as the chick stripped out the mink, revealing a phenomenally shaped body.

"What?!" the chick asked, unsure if she'd done something wrong.

"Tie them motherfuckers up! That's what!" Nanfu answered her then mushed her ass to the floor to show her he meant business.

"What's your name, snow bunny?" York asked her.

"Silvia," she replied.

"Well, Silvia, hurry the fuck up! We ain't got all day," York added, as he watched Silvia scramble to comply. It didn't take long for her to bind up her family and cover their faces with the pillowcases.

"I-I'm done," Silvia announced tentatively, as she sat on her knees, looking up into her kidnappers' faces.

"No, you're not! Now, we have some fun. Yo, York, toss the living room and kitchen. And you... you're gonna show

me everything in this home worth stealing. Cause if you don't... you'll watch me fuck your girl in the ass before I put a bullet in her skull," Nanfu said, as he snatched Silvia onto her feet. "Now come on, bitch. The sooner you're done, the sooner we'll leave," Nanfu added, as he pushed Silvia ahead of him and led her to what had to be her bedroom.

Meanwhile, York was in the living room, wrecking shit.

"No antiques... No precious family heirlooms. All these fuckers have is some funky ass Billy Joel and Hall and Oats tapes," York sniped, as he flung the tapes across the room. With no luck in finding anything valuable, York exited the living room and headed for the kitchen. "Fucking yodies. Brotha can't pawn no fucking candleholders," York griped, as he went through the pantry cabinets. "Now that's what's up!" York stated, as his eyes fell upon a sure treat.

Back in the master bedroom, things were going good as well. Silvia was moving like a woman possessed, as she flung all her minks into Nanfu's trash bag and then, she dashed to her vanity set and chucked every piece of jewelry she owned into the bag as well.

"Where's the safe?" Nanfu asked Silvia, as she looked around the room, scanning for anything else of value she could offer.

"Safe?" Silvia phrased the word like a question and gazed at Nanfu quizzically.

"You think this shit a game?!" Nanfu growled at Silvia then cocked the hammer of his .357 and aimed at her face.

"Middle shelf... of the closet. It-it pulls out. B-but I don't know the code."

"Then you've got one minute to get the code. And I mean one minute," Nanfu said, as he lowered the gun and okayed her to go retrieve the code.

Moments later, she ran into the room and went to work opening the safe. "You know you fucked up; don't cha?!" Nanfu stated, as Silvia worked the combination to the safe.

"How... I-I mean I'm sorry," Silvia pleaded.

"Save your breath. Once you get that safe open, I'll deal with you."

Click.

The safe opened to reveal a jewelry box full of precious family heirlooms and almost $70,000 in cash. "Jackpot!" Nanfu exclaimed, as he tossed the contents of the safe into the bag. Once everything had been removed from the safe and the bag was tied, the room grew very quiet. Silvia stood in front of Nanfu and only a few steps from her bed. Nanfu was a big nigga. At 6'2", he towered over Silvia's 5'4" frame. Nanfu was shaped like Ving Rhames and rocked the bald head as well. He stood looking Silvia over from head to toe. She visibly trembled, as Nanfu continued to undress her with his eyes.

Oh, my God! He's gonna screw me, Silvia thought to herself. She trembled again when she realized that instead of fear, she felt a strange sense of arousal. Her pussy began to lube itself, as her clit started to throb, causing her nipples to grow extremely erect.

What the fuck?! This bitch nipples are getting hard, Nanfu thought, as he focused on her silk blouse.

"Please don't... rape me," Silvia said in a tone that sounded more like she was hoping he'd fuck her to Nanfu.

"Take off your clothes... Don't make me ask twice," Nanfu stated, as he waved the .357 at her.

Silvia did as she was told and stripped all the way down to her silk undergarments. Her breasts were full C-cups, and her belly was a flat slope that led to the mother of all camel toes. Nanfu's mouth almost dropped open, as he noticed the bulge within Silvia's panties. Damn... Either this bitch got a dick or she phatter than a motherfucker, Nanfu thought, as he regained his composure and threw back on his screw face. "Take them panties off," Nanfu ordered Silvia in a tone far too sensual to be harsh.

As this was taking place, York busied himself enjoying the treasure he'd found, which was a box of Captain Crunch cereal. And with the biggest bowl he could find, he'd emptied the box into the bowl and was munching his hungry little ass off, as he walked down the hall toward Nanfu's location. When York gazed into the room and saw Silvia stepping out of her panties, he damn near choked on the cereal he was chewing. "Bra! What the hell's going on?" York asked, not sure if his eyes were playing tricks on him or not.

"Be easy, youngblood. We just gone teach little miss hot ass some manners," Nanfu said, as he turned Silvia toward the bed and slung her onto it face first. Nanfu pinned her chest to the bed by placing his forearm into her back. "Yo, York! Grab this bitch's legs. If she squirms or bucks, snatch her off the bed by her feet," Nanfu stated, as he took his loose hand and pulled off his belt. York put down the bowl of cereal and grabbed Silvia by her calves. No sooner than York grabbed her legs, Nanfu firmly popped Silvia's ass with the belt.

"Ungh! Ow!" Silvia yelped in startled pain, but she didn't squirm nor buck.

"That was for Nat Turner..."

Pop!

"That's for Malcolm."

Pop-Pop-Pop!

"That's for Harriet Tubman and Langston Hughes!" Nanfu yelled out to Silvia after each time he'd whipped her ass.

"Hold up, bro. I'll do the shit talking. You pop the ass," York said to Nanfu, who nodded in approval and recommenced the spanking.

Pop-Pop!

"Augh! Oww!" Silvia squealed in pain.

"Bitch, shut up. That's for all the Black people you motherfuckers hung from trees like human piñatas!"

Pop-Pop-Pop-Pop!

"That's for crossing the street every time you see me coming up the same side of the block," York said, venting his *frustrations, as Nanfu continued to whip Silvia. This continued until Silvia pissed on herself and passed out from the beating she had taken. After tying Silvia up and washing the bowl York had eaten from, they both exited the building, the huge bag of goods in tow, and a dilemma arose.*

"Hey! Hey, you two!" yelled one of the security guards, as he rose from the lobby security desk and approached them.

"Fuck!" York exclaimed just loud enough for Nanfu to hear.

"Be easy. I got this," Nanfu stated, as he took one of his hands off the bag and reached for his .357.

"You guys need some help?" the guard asked, as he drew closer.

"Yeah! Could you grab the door for us?" Nanfu suggested, as he used his head to motion the guard toward the front door.

"Sure," the guard replied. Within moments, the two were out of the building with the stolen goods secured. The two sat at a light three blocks away, laughing hysterically.

"Can you believe that?! The guard actually helped us rob them muthafuckers," Nanfu stated. causing them to burst into another bout of hysterical laughter.

"York! Yo, York!" Animal yelled, snapping York out of his thoughts.

"Huh?! Yeah! What's up?" York replied, somewhat startled, as he turned and looked upon Animal, as he resettled into the passenger seat of the Range.

"Not shit!" Animal replied, as he shut the door of the Range and reached for his seatbelt.

"So, your mistress hadn't heard anything?" York asked, as he re-ignited the engine.

"My what?! She's just..." Animal began his lie, but the look written over York's face said, "Negro, please."

"Nah, she didn't know nothing. But she did have a spot for us to check out. You know where Daryl's Barbershop is, right?" Animal asked in an 'everyone knows that spot' type of tone. York nodded and pulled away from the curb. "Kiyanna thinks Chase is creeping on his 'ol lady with some girl who stays near the shop," Animal added, as York merely nodded to indicate he had heard him. "If we lucky, we might be able to catch the nigga with his pants down," Animal stated, seeking to coax a reply from York.

One can only hope, York thought to himself, as he cut his eyes at Animal then returned his focus to the road without uttering a response.

The barbershop was, as most were in the hood, abuzz with an array of people. Some old guys in the back corner were playing checkers, while the rest of the shop's patrons appeared to be blue collar workers or lower-level dope pushers. Daryl, the owner, wasn't there, but Moochie, the gossip loving, lead barber, was. Animal sat in Moochie's chair, as the gossipy barber began speaking on random dirt. York chose to take a standing position by the shop's entrance, watching the block for Chase.

"Look, you muthasucka, you not gonna cheat me," said a Nigerian named Lukumom who was fussing over a chess move with Chestnut, the shop owner's uncle.

Some things never change, York thought, as he turned from the ongoing squabble and found himself looking into the face of a not too old and very familiar friend. Her name was Michelle and never had York met a chick quite like her. And because or her unique form, York had given her the name Fifty. York started to move toward the shop's entrance but was halted when Michelle spotted him and gave him the signal to 'hold up'. No sooner than she gave the signal, her mom appeared on the block with a little toddler in tow. The little girl couldn't be much older than three, and from the way the child embraced Michelle, it was obvious that the little girl was hers.

York turned his back on them to avoid being seen by Michelle's mom. The woman never cared much for York and had no problem letting him know this. Any time she caught York and Michelle, she broke fool. And today, York was in no mood for her drama. *So, Ms. Fifty's a mom! Hmph!* York thought to himself, as he smirked and allowed his growing erection to lead him down another trip into the past.

Knock-Knock-Knock!

"Yo, keep pushing. Animal, don't let this nigga off the bench without finishing his rep," York stated, as he left Animal spotting Lopez, who was having a tough time with his bench pressing. The three of them were in the converted storage room of the building they hustled out of. The three of them had turned the room into their own gym/chill spot. But visitors, unless brought down by them, were not allowed. And every tenant in the building knew this rule. At least York had thought so.

Knock-Knock-Bam-Bam-Bam!

"Open the fucking door… Gone tell me to come holla… I know you hear me, nigga," a female voice yelled from behind the door. At first, York thought the voice was that of his lady, Stephanie, but knew this couldn't be because she had left earlier to spend the night with her cousin in Camden, N.J.

So, who the fuck is this?! York thought, as he opened the door to solve the mystery.

"So, a girl gotta show her ass to get some attention around here, huh?!" Michelle said as soon as the door flung open.

"Do it and watch your ass get broke off real proper," York replied, as he smiled from ear to ear and moved aside to let Michelle enter the room.

"Oh, hell nah! I know that wasn't you going bonkers on the door!"

"Shut your mouth, nigga! Always acting hard. You're scared of pussy too!" Michelle flung the words at Animal.

"Oooo!" York and Lopez said in unison as Animal's mouth flew open in shock.

"And what you oooo-ing for? You too pretty for some real pussy!" Michelle said to Lopez, causing both Animal and York to double over in tears, laughing.

"I'm not... You don't... We the mad boners." Lopez fumbled out the wors, as Michelle rolled her eyes at him and turned her back on him and Animal to face York.

"Mad boners?! Yeah, right! I can't tell! Y'all quick to fuck those poor in the ass, slack breasted bitches. But scared to fuck with this..." Michelle said, as she took her hands and placed them on her forty-two-inch ass and slowly rubbed it, as she looked York in the eyes. "Maybe I'm too thick for you... Maybe cause I'm blessed with the best," Michelle stated then moaned as she slid her left hand up and under her T-shirt while sliding her right hand down into the crotch of her cashmere sweatpants. York's dick was harder than re-enforced steel, as he watched Michelle saunter over to the weight bench. "Maybe I'm just too much woman for you mad boners..." she stated, as she kicked off her house slippers and lay down on her back across the bench, locking eyes with Animal, who stood hovering above her head. Michelle lifted her legs into the air and began removing her sweatpants. It was graveyard quiet, as Michelle stood again and bent over, touching her toes for no reason other than to show off her pretty pussy. Lopez and Animal had the perfect view of her well-trimmed pussy until she kicked away her sweatpants and dropped down to the floor in a full split.

"Damn!" All three of the guys exclaimed, as they watched Michelle bounce half up and back down into a full split three times. A chick doing splits wasn't anything normally seen as special. But when done by Michelle, a nigga had no choice but to stand in awe. Michelle, somewhere between her first and third bounce, had flung off her t-shirt, exposing two of the hugest, fullest, most incredibly perfect tits York had ever seen.

"Hmph! I guess I was right. You guys really are scared," Michelle stated, as she rose and kneeled on the bench.

Michelle hoisted her ass into the air and rested her elbow on the bench. "I wonder what does a girl gotta..."

Z-i-ip!

The sound of opening zippers silenced Michelle.

"Don't stop talking now," York said, as Michelle looked over her shoulder to find a butt naked York approaching her coochie with his dick in his hand.

"Gawd damn!" Animal yelped out, as the pleasure he received from Michelle's mouth locked his legs. This was all the cue York needed. Without further ado, York slid every inch of his dick in her cunt, causing Michelle to half choke on Animal's dick.

"What's the matter, Chelle?! Can't take the dick? Huh?!" York stated, as he slid all the way out and rammed himself all the way back into her cunt.

"Ungh! Ooh! Ungh!" Michelle groaned and moaned and choked, as her pussy and mouth continued being stuffed by cocks.

"Yo, let a nigga get some shine. Y'all niggas straight handcuffing the pussy," Lopez griped, as he held his dick, craving some action.

"Yo-York! Move..." Michelle said, as she reached back to push York out of her pussy.

"Yo, what the fuck?!" York protested, as he pulled out of Michelle's cunt.

"Chill, bae... Phew! You just too much. I gotta be one on one with you," Michelle said, as she turned and lay on her back, spreading her legs and opening her mouth to entice the guys to resume their invasions. Lopez dove into her pussy with the quickness, as York dropped his dick into Chelle's mouth before Animal could beat him to the punch. "Mmm!" Michelle moaned, as she gave and received pleasure.

"Hold her legs. I'm trying to put my balls in this broad," Lopez said, as he watched York and Animal sit down and each grab a leg.

"Ungh! Oh-oh! Yeah! Yeah, bae!" Michelle moaned, as Lopez put in work, pumping dick into her puffy wet pussy.

"That's right! Moan, muthafucker! I thought… I was… too pretty for… some pus-pusss-sseee-ee!" Lopez tried to shit talk

But Michelle reached up and gripped him around the shoulders. As soon as her hands locked onto his flesh, Michelle began slinging her pussy like her ass was on fire. A pussy slinger with some bomb ass coochie was the last woman you wanted to talk shit to. Lopez was now finding this out. "Nah, uh-uh. Don't scream now, nigga!" Michelle stated. as she pumped her pussy on Lopez's dick. Lopez was in trouble. He had shit talked the wrong woman. And now, he stood in front of his crew, using every ounce of his might to keep himself from screaming like a bitch. "What's wrong, huh, nigga?! Pussy got you fucked up, don't it?! Uh-huh! Well, you gone love this!" Michelle stated, as she locked her lips onto the nape of Lopez's neck and sucked with all her might, all the while steadily flinging her coochie uncontrollably. The combination was too much for Lopez to handle.

"Ooh-ahh-h! Oooh!" Lopez screamed out, as he jumped off the pussy and creamed all down the side of Michelle's thighs.

"Damn, son! The pussy that good?" Animal asked York, who was busy replacing his dick down Michelle's throat. "Fuck this!" Animal pushed Lopez aside. "Hold them legs," Animal instructed Lopez, as he popped the head of his dick into Michelle, who had only one more obstacle standing in the way of her long-awaited one-on-one session with York… Animal. Michelle did the same with Animal as she had done with Lopez. She moaned louder for Animal than she had for Lopez. She needed Animal to believe he was better at fucking her than Lopez was. So, she pretended to jump in pain when she felt Animal's pelvic bone smack against her coochie. Next, she focused on Animal's sex game. Lopez was a rabbit

humper. In and out, in and out. No technique whatsoever. But Animal was a grinder. He liked to try and hit every corner of a pussy – or at least break his dick trying. But with years of gymnastics under her belt, Michelle knew just the way to handle Animal.

"Ungh! Yo, Chelle, chill," York grunted out, as she squeezed his balls, causing him to drop her leg.

Michelle smiled, loving how her plan was coming together. She wrapped her loose leg around Animal's left hip and focused herself on tightening up her cunt. It didn't take long for Animal to feel the effects. Michelle knew she had him fucked up when she saw Animal's jaw tighten and his eyes twitch. York was complaining about her stopping the blow job, but she ignored him and focused harder on milking Animal's cock. When she felt Animal's body tense then tremble, Michelle smiled.

"Yeah, muthafucker! Can't hang! Huh?!" she proclaimed, as she kept her cunt tight and began throwing that pussy on Animal.

"Oo-oo-oo-oo-sh-shit!" Animal yelped like a bitch, as he bucked and jumped around like he was doing the Humpty Dance. Animal skeeted all over the floor beneath the bench and stumbled out the pussy before falling to the floor on one knee.

"Damn!" York and Lopez said in unison then burst into laughter after watching Animal get broke down by some pussy.

"What's so funny, York?! It's your turn," Michelle stated, as she rose off the bench and signaled for York to lay on it.

"Nah! Fuck that bench. Me and you gone hit the floor," York said, as he rounded the bench to approach her.

"Bench... the floor... it don't matter. Just bring it!" Michelle said, as she moved a huge futon from the corner of the room. By the time York got near Michelle, she was using the futon as a makeshift pillow with the rest of her body lying on some blankets. Looking up at York, Michelle gave him her

best fuck slut look and parted her legs as wide as she could. "Bring it," Michelle said, as York kneeled down between her legs. Finally, Michelle thought, as she realized she was about to achieve her goal to bed York. Michelle knew all about the reputation of York and his mad boners crew and had tried for over a year to get next to York. Finally, she broke past his barriers and became chummy with him. She had even started her own personal touchy-feely game with him. This morning when she'd ground her ass against his zipper, he had got very hard. And when she reached back and gripped it through his jeans, he'd told her to "stop by sometime."

"Umm!" Michelle moaned in delight, as York began to slide his cock in her hot and slick cunt. Yes, she was going to enjoy this visit. "York. Oo-oh, York!" she moaned, as he held her legs wide while slowly guiding all his dick into her.

"Aw, look at this nigga!"

"This nigga trying to make love."

"Don't hate cause his dick game... ungh! Oo-o! Is-is better than ya-ya-alls!" Michelle moaned out her statement that silenced Animal and Lopez while encouraging York to keep doing what he was doing. And that was exactly what he did.

York slow pumped the pussy and looked her in the eyes the entire time. Then, when Michelle's coochie started painting his dick white with her cum, York leaned down and took the nipple of one of her 531 breasts and wrapped his mouth around it. York circled, nibbled, and licked that chocolate nub of a nipple in such a way that Michelle's clit began to spasm, causing her cunt to drench York's cock with even more cum.

"Uh-oo-ooh!" Michelle moaned from the depths of her soul, as York rose to his knees and pinned her ankles to the futon. With both of Michelle's ankles and legs pinned along each side of her head, York closed his eyes and dropped the hammer on her cunt.

"Ah-ooh-ooh-oow!" Michelle screamed, as York's first vicious thrust sent waves of pleasure pulsing through her entire body.

"That's what you want?! That's how you like it?! Talk to Daddy! Tell me where you want this dick!" York stated, as he pumped long dick to Michelle.

"Ooh! Fu-Fuck!" she moaned, as York proved to be everything Michelle thought he would be and more.

"Ungh-Ye-Yeah! Ooh! Fuck!" York exclaimed, as his balls shot out a full clip of nut.

"York! Yo-York! You alright?!" Michelle asked, snapping York out of his lewd flashback.

"Huh?! Oh, hey! How you doing, Fifty?" York asked after recovering from being caught off guard.

"I'm good. Sorry bout earlier. But you and my mom just don't mix. And I…"

"Yo, York! No one's seen him," Animal said, cutting Michelle off.

"Well, fuck you too! Mr. Humpty!" Michelle stated snappishly, causing her and York to erupt into laughter.

"I'll be out in the car," Animal grumbled at them then exited the shop.

"What's wrong with him?" Michelle asked, as she slid closer to York.

"Nothing for you to worry over. We just having a tough time catching this nigga who shot my man."

"That was your people involved in that Rockefeller shit?!"

"Yeah! So, what's the word around here?" York asked.

"Except for the scoop on what went down, nothing much," she replied.

"Hmph! You know any guy named Chase? He reps Redfern?" York asked, not expecting much from Michele.

"Why? He shot your man?" Michelle asked.

"Don't know. But I think he may know who did it," York replied.

"What the fuck they yapping about?" Animal said to himself, as he watched them through the shop window from the car. Animal was growing more tense. The longer they stayed around the shop, the more likely they were to run into Chase. And with Animal still needing time to stall York, hanging around this hood wasn't what he needed. "Hell yeah! That's what's up!" Animal mumbled to himself, as he watched York kiss Michelle on the cheek and wave goodbye. "Damn, nigga! What Chelle say to you that got you cheesing like that?" Animal asked York, as he hopped back behind the wheel.

"Remember Wet Pussy?"

"Best dick sucker in Jamaica Queens Wet Pussy?!" Animal replied, somewhat confused.

"Yeah! Apparently, Chase knows her too," York answered then cranked up the Range and steered it toward Wet Pussy's crib.

***

As York and Animal parked the Range Rover in front of the PJs where Wet Pussy resided, she was busy upstairs trying to calm down Chase.

"You know you never did tell me how you came across Wet Pussy," Animal stated, as he walked alongside York toward the building stoop.

"And I never will," York replied definitively, as he opened the entrance door for Animal and was engulfed by more memories from his past. It had been almost five years since York had brought Animal and Lopez to meet his queen freak. Her name was Angela, but York and the many men who'd fucked her called her Wet Pussy. York had given her the name due to the fact that her coochie stayed wet and ready to fuck. Always! If there was a name for something worse that a nympho, Wet Pussy was that. York had only brought Lopez and Animal to her crib once, and this was because she swore she could fuck York and at least two more guys until their balls were drained and still not be satisfied. York dared her to show and prove. And Wet Pussy accepted the challenge. As soon as the guys walked in, before York could close the door to her crib, it was on.

"Damn!" both Lopez and Animal proclaimed, as their eyes roamed over Wet Pussy's completely naked body.

"I'm sure York told y'all what's up. So, strip off your clothes. Go into the living room and get ready to have your balls drained," Wet Pussy stated then headed down the hallway to a back bedroom.

"Oh, shit, son! You wasn't playing!" Animal stated, as he fumbled with his pants.

"And the bitch fly as fuck. Yo, what's the catch?! How much we gotta peel out?" Lopez stated skeptically.

"What's the hold up?! My pussy's on fire! Let's fuck!" Wet Pussy stated, as she walked back into the living room. The words she uttered sent the three men's hormones into overdrive. Clothes began being chucked all over the room, as Wet Pussy stood in the middle of all three men and feasted her eyes upon their naked flesh. Wet Pussy stood about 5'5" and weighed about one hundred thirty-five pounds. She was one hundred percent Puerto Rican and possessed a body men would kill for. She had full C-cup breasts and a butt that would put J. Lo to shame. She had lips like Angelina Jolie, and her eyes were green as jade. She sported a Toni Braxton hair style that complemented the "I'll fuck the shit out of you" expression written all over her face. With the guys now all nude and aroused, Wet Pussy instructed Animal and Lopez to sit side by side on the couch. She guided York to her rear then got down on her knees and gripped Animal and Lopez's dicks.

"Come on, Daddy! You know what I want," Wet Pussy said, looking over her shoulder at York. But before he could lower himself behind her, she turned her head forward and began sucking dick.

"Ah-oo-mmm!" Lopez groaned in pleasure, as Wet Pussy worked his dick phenomenally with her tongue, lips, and hand.

"Oo-uww-mm!" Wet Pussy moaned over Lopez's cock, as York slid his dick balls deep into her slickened coochie. The skills of her head game was second to none. And soon, Lopez found himself squiring, trying to pry his cock from Wet Pussy's mouth.

"Damn, son! Stop whining!" Animal jokingly commented then burst into laughter. But his words fell upon deaf ears, as Lopez gave into the pleasure he was receiving.

"Ooh-ooh-ahh-ooo!" Lopez screamed like a scalded cat, as his dick poured hot cum all down Wet Pussy's throat. Although Lopez flinched and bucked all over the place while he was skeeting spunk, not a single solitary drop went unswallowed by Wet Pussy: She sucked and slurped Lopez's cock until all traces of cum were gone, leaving his dick wet and shriveled from being drained. York could only smirk, as he knew all too well just how powerless one was when receiving head from Wet Pussy. Wasting no time, Wet Pussy shifted over from Lopez to center her mouth above Animal's cock, but before she wrapped her lips around his dick, she reached back with her right hand and pulled her butt cheeks apart. "My ass, Daddy! Fuck me in the ass slow and nasty," Wet Pussy moaned out the request then dove throat first onto Animal's cock.

"Claud-hav-mmm!" Animal yelped out, as Wet Pussy's technique sent pleasure all through his body.

"Okay! Mamacita!" York said, as he rubbed cunt juice all over Wet Pussy's anus to lube it for his dick's entry.

"Mmm! Oow! Mmm!" Wet Pussy hummed on the head of Animal's cock, as York pushed his dick into her tight asshole. Then, without warming, something popped – or felt like it popped when York was pushing into her ass. Whatever it was, it instantly flipped a switch inside of Wet Pussy. "Oh-my-ooh-sh-sh-shit! Aww-fuck!" Wet Pussy wailed, as she

pushed her face from Animal's cock then stumbled backwards and fell on top of York's chest. All the while, York's cock stayed lodged in Wet Pussy's ass.

All this recollecting took place as York and Animal ascended the stairs leading up to Wet Pussy's apartment. She was busy trying to relieve and pry open the mind of her agitated company.

"Chase, you gotta calm down. You should be safe here. York hasn't been over to see me in over a year. So, sit; relax, and tell me what's going on," Wet Pussy stated, as she sat Chase down and tried to get to the bottom of the shit he was in.

"I told you. I got word from my crew to keep it moving if I came across anyone from the Wolfpack Cartel. Something happened over at Rockefeller Plaza. And since we've always had beef, I just don't think it's smart to be anywhere around any of them."

"And you've done nothing to piss them off?" Wet Pussy asked in a blatantly skeptical tone.

"No! I haven't! I-I… Fuck it! I don't care what you think. But I will tell you this much. I'm getting tired of all this damn running. As soon as my crew get here, we gone handle this shit."

"Now don't go and do something stupid. You'll fuck around and make a bad problem worse. What you need to do…"

Knock-Knock-Knock!

The banging at her door cut Wet Pussy's suggestion to Chase short.

"Who dat?!" Chase asked suspiciously, as he rose off the couch.

"Boy, calm down!" Wet Pussy replied, as she went to answer her door.

Chase looked around his immediate surroundings for an emergency escape should one be needed. He eyed the living room's lone window which led to the apartment's fire escape and smiled.

Knock-Knock-Knock!

"Hey, hey, hey! I'm coming!" Wet Pussy yelled, as she peeped out the peephole. But whomever her visitors were, they had their finger covering the peephole. "Alright! Who playing with my door?" Wet Pussy yelled out, a bit agitated.

"Hey, Chunky Monkey!" York replied, keeping his finger covering the door's peephole.

"Oh, shit! It's York! Nigga, what you done got me into?!" Wet Pussy said accusingly.

"Shit! Stall him!" Chase blurted out.

"What... Who is this?!' she yelled through the door once more.

"I said, 'Hey Chucky Monkey!'" York yelled once more.

"Who is this?! Gimme a name!" Wet Pussy stated.

"Oh, hell no! Kick in the door," York ordered, as he took his loose hand and drew his .44 caliber.

Tha-oom-aloom-a-loom!

Animal kicked the door off its hinges and directly on top of Wet Pussy.

Chase didn't see but heard the door get kicked in, as he hopped through the window and onto the fire escape. York entered through the threshold with gun in hand and Animal on his heels. Wet Pussy rolled from under the kicked in door and found herself face-to-face with the wrong end of the gun.

"Oohh, my God!" Wet Pussy exclaimed, as she tried to crawl backwards away from the barrel of the gun.

"State my name?!" *Click!* "State my name!" York barked out the words, as he pulled the hammer back on his .44 caliber and aimed the barrel at her chest.

"York, chill!" Animal said, as he jumped between York and Wet Pussy.

"Angela, where is he?" York asked through clenched teeth. York hated to be played, and he really hated for anyone to play on his intelligence, which was what Wet Pussy had been doing when he'd knocked on her door.

"Where's who?!" Wet Pussy continued to play dumb as she replied.

"Bitch, you think this a game?!" York yelled then snatched her up by her arm and buried the barrel into her cheek.

"Oh, shit!" Chase gasped out then scrambled down the fire escape.

"What the..." Animal blurted out then dashed toward the window, looking out the fire escape. Wet Pussy dropped back to the floor, as York let her loose and followed Animal's lead.

Pop-Pop!

"Fuck! He getting away!" Animal griped, as he fired twice but missed his target. Animal bolted from the window and began to run toward the crib's front entrance.

"How you gone trip when I haven't seen you in over a year? You don't own this pussy," she blanked, as York went to the window to pop the scene.

"You think this about..." York began his statement then held his breath, trying to quench his rage. 'That fun-dummy you fucking shot one of my wolves. Or knows who did. And until I figure out which it is, you may wanna find you some new dick," York stated, as he turned and ran from the crib.

Meanwhile, Chase had managed to reach the bottom of the fire escape and was wasting no time exiting the side alley of the building he'd just vacated.

"Keep your eyes open for York. Word is he's running through hoods, wrecking shit," Von warned Sharrod, who was riding shotgun.

"I don't see York, but I do see Chase," Sharrod said, as he pointed out Chase to Von. Chase had just emerged from an alley about a half black ahead of Von's pearl white Ford Mustang, and the odd way Chase was scanning the block caused Von and Sharrod to instantly raise their own guard.

"Get his attention," Von stated to Sharrod, as he honked the car's horn.

"Yo! Yo, Chase!" Sharrod yelled up the block at Chase, as he hopped out the passenger side of the Mustang.

"Oh, fuck!" Chase blurted out, as he assumed the man who had yelled out his name was someone watching the block for York.

Chase quickly turned to head up the block away from his assumed threat. Before he could take five steps, Animal stepped out on the stoop of the building Chase had not yet fled from.

"Fuck!" Chase yelled, as he drew his piece from his waist and ducked between two nearby parked cars.

"York! He's out here!" Animal screamed out, as he aimed his .9mm toward Chase. *Pop-Pop-Pop-Pop!* "Fuck!" Animal blurted out, as bullets tore into the concrete base of the stoop. Animal ducked then dove back into the hallway of the building's entrance. "Get down!" Animal blurted out, as he damn near knocked over York, who was dashing toward the front stoop.

"Move! This nigga wants war?!" York said, as he moved toward the entrance's threshold and peeked around it to scan the block. Sharrod had crept up the block and circled behind Chase. Chase, unsure of who had shot at Animal, had crouched under a Range Rover for cover.

"Come on, son! We gotta bounce," Sharrod stated, as he tugged on a balled up and frightened Chase.

"Sh-Sharrod! Where's Von?" Chase asked, as he crawled from under the Range Rover.

"Waiting down there... go ahead... I gotcha covered," Sharrod replied, as he popped up behind the hood of the Range Rover after pointing Chase in the right direction. York spotted the moving men near his Range Rover and had already aimed his .44 caliber in the direction of the SUV. As soon as Sharrod popped up, York let loose.

Boom!

"Augh!" Sharrod screamed, as the bullet ripped through his shoulder, knocking him back on his ass.

"What the fuck?!" Von blurted out, as he flinched behind the wheel of the Mustang and threw the car's gear into reverse.

"Cover me!" York ordered Animal then dashed off the stoop. Animal used the threshold for cover, as he watched York circle around the hood of the car parked in front of his Range Rover. As soon as York cleared the vehicle, his gun was spitting.

Boom-Boom!

The first bullet tore a hole into the concrete, forcing Chase to dash behind the Rover and tear ass down the block, while the second bullet ripped through Sharrod's thigh as he attempted to flee.

"Awww! Fuck-k!" Sharrod screamed in pain, as he dropped to the ground once more.

"Man, fuck this!" Von stated to himself then floored the Mustang, as he peeled off in reverse.

"Yo! Hold up! Yo, Von!" Chase yelled out and waved his hands frantically, trying to get Von to stop for him, but it was to no avail. Von wasn't stopping.

"Yo, you shot my man?!" York asked Sharrod, as he kicked away Sharrod's gun and aimed at Sharrod's chest.

"I-I swear it..."

"Yo, they're getting away!' Animal yelled out to York, cutting off Sharrod's reply.

"See what this nigga knows!" York stated to Animal, as he motioned him toward Sharrod and sprinted down the block after Chase. Chase had almost a full block lead on York, and once Chase caught sight of York, his feet went to working double time.

"Fuck all this running," York said to himself and aimed his .44 at the center of Chase's fleeing frame. But before he could pull the trigger, Chase ran off the sidewalk and sprinted across the street. The cars that lined the street blocked York from being able to get off a clear shot. "Fuck!" York exclaimed, as he moved off the sidewalk to get a better angle. But by the time York got around the cars and re-drew his gun, Chase was cutting down a side street, once again denying York any chance to let off a shot.

Boom-Boom!

The shot momentarily startled York, but since they had come from behind him, York figured they had to have come from Animal's gun.

"Yo, Animal! Animal!"

"Yo!" Animal shouted as a reply to York's call.

"Here... Take the keys and get the Range," York stated, as he implied for Animal to follow him, as he resumed his pursuit of Chase.

Animal scooped up the keys York had tossed onto the street and sprinted back toward the Range, as York took off down the side street Chase had dashed down. As soon as York booked down the side street, he stopped in his tracks and began shaking his head in frustration.

"Talk about luck of the Irish!" York sarcastically mumbled to himself, as he watch every housing unit being prepped for what looked to be a block party. Everywhere he looked, girls were sweeping stoops or setting out chairs. Guys were carrying crates of vinyl records and other various DJing equipment, while the women on the block were towing groceries and boxes of sodas and beers.

"Of all the blocks a nigga could choose to run down, this nigga had to choose one throwing a block party," York said to himself, as he realized Chase could be anywhere on the block and still avoid detection. With this point in mind, York stood still and considered his odds. *If Chase is still on this block, he could be anywhere. He could also be strapped. And if he's strapped, he could be laying in a cut somewhere waiting to peel my wig,* York thought to himself, as he continued scanning the block.

"Hey, York! York! Over here!" Daytona yelled out from a nearby stoop, as he motioned for York to join him.

"You heard anything new?" York asked Daytona, as he climbed the stairs of the stoop.

"Nothing that I haven't already told you," Daytona replied, as he and York side-stepped to allow a woman towing groceries to enter the building. At that time, Animal crept down the block, looking for York.

"Aww, fuck!" Animal cursed, as he spotted York on the stoop with Daytona.

"What you doing over here? I thought you'd be busy wrecking shop in the Bronx," Daytona said to York, as he spotted Animal parking York's Range Rover.

"The Bronx?! What the Bronx got to do with this?" York replied, looking bewildered.

"It's got everything to do with this. Them niggas that clapped Zahir…"

"Niggas? All I got was one name," York stated, cutting off Daytona's comments.

"I gave Animal the names of the men who shot Zahir and their girlfriends' names as well. The way I see it, if they was hired to pull this lick or acted alone, one of they girls would know or at least know somebody who might know," Daytona stated.

"I spoke with Chase's girl, and she didn't seem to know much," York replied, as he glanced at the block.

"Chase! Who the hell is that?"

"Animal said you told him Chase was down with the nigga who shot Zahir."

"It was some young guns outta the Bronx. Bullet, Hammer, and Shell."

"What?! Shell? Bullet?" York stated in a confused tone.

"Hey, don't look at me. That's what them niggas called themselves. But that's my word. I told Animal everything I just told you," Daytona stated, seeking to clarity the mix up.

"So, Chase ain't got nothing to do with this?" York asked, seeking to find any way Animal could have come to assume Chase might have been involved.

"Not according to my sources. But if you tell me what hood to check, I can ask around," Daytona suggested.

"Naw, I'm good. But if you hear anything else about them Bronx niggas, let me know," York stated, as he turned to exit the stoop.

"Bet! Yo, if you heading to the Bronx, be careful. Them niggas know what went down and how you roll. They shook on how the cartel might respond. So, everyone with a strap is probably strapped," Daytona stated, attempting to give York the heads up.

"I would imagine they are. But I got more important fish to fry. Call me when you know something more," York replied, as he descended the stairs of the stoop and approached his Range Rover.

"So, what's the word?" Animal asked York, as he hopped out the driver's side of the Range and circled the hood to hop into the passenger seat.

"I don't know… You tell me," York stated, as he hopped behind the wheel of the Range and looked Animal square in the eyes. Tension filled the air between them.

Moments passed without a single word spoken. Animal's face told nothing. But for a split second, Animal's eyes slipped up, but he recovered just as quickly as he had slipped. "What you mean?" Animal answered.

Animal's reply let York know that whatever Animal was hiding wasn't going to be revealed willingly. York would need something concrete enough to compel Animal to fess up. With this in mind, York played the only card he currently held in hand. "Sharrod!? What did he know?" York asked Animal in a tone that said, 'Nigga, what do you think I'm talking about?' Animal's heart fell to his feet then jumped into his throat, as he rushed to both hide his relief and supply York with an answer.

"He wanted to play dumb, so I put two into his dome to help him remember," Animal replied.

"Hmph!" York stated then glanced over at the console to check the time. It was 2:43 p.m. *By now, I should've been closer to the truth. But instead, I'm farther away,* York mentally assessed, as he stared expressionlessly at the console.

"So, what's our next move?" Animal asked, cutting off York's thoughts.

"Nothing! There is no next move," York replied, as he shifted the Range Rover's gear into drive and pulled off.

"What?! Are you serious? What about Chase?" Animal asked.

"What about him?" York answered, as he programmed the Range's navigational system to find the quickest route to Mt. Sinai.

"He shot Zahir! The muthafucker clapped our man!" Animal proclaimed in a somewhat bewildered tone.

"Are you sure? Can you prove Chase shot Zahir?" York calmly replied.

"I can't believe this shit! We've been driving all around Queens, looking for this nigga. Now you just wanna…"

"Be easy, fam. Chase or whoever shot Zahir gone feel it. But right now, we gone chill. We gonna swing by the hospital, check on Zahir status. Then, I'm going home to get me something to eat," York stated, cutting off Animal's protest.

'So, that's it?! We just gone chill?!" Animal questioned sarcastically.

"I think we should wait to see if Zahir makes it out of surgery. I'd like to know what he remembers about being shot. So, until I know more about Zahir's chances of surviving surgery, I say we chill. Understood?!" York stated in a tone that dared Animal to challenge him.

"Yeah," Animal replied, as York reached over to turn on the stereo.

Something just ain't right. Something just ain't mutha-fucking right, York thought to himself, as he and Animal drove the rest of the way to the hospital in silence.

***

"We gotta kill him. I don't know how we gonna do it. But it gotta be done," Animal said, as he spoke to Drea on his cell phone.

"Killing York ain't nothing, baby. All you gotta do is…"

"What the fuck is wrong with you?! When did York's name come out my mouth? When?!" Animal snapped, cutting off Drea's comments.

"It didn't! But it should. The muthafucker wants to wait until he speak with Zahir before he makes another move. How does that not constitute a problem?" Drea stated, seeking to justify her opinion.

"York's not a threat. At least not yet," Animal replied.

"But baby, can't you see?! That's why we need to take him out now. Before it's too late. Imagine the chaos York's death would cause…" Drea reasoned. "With York dead, no one will be thinkin' about Zahir no more. Everyone in the cartel will be focused on finding York's killer."

"*No!*" Animal stated, cutting off Drea's persuasion.

"But baby, with everyone watching over Zahir, who's to stop us from killing him?"

"I said *no*! Our problem is Zahir, not York. So, get your mind off York and focus on how we gone kill Zahir," Animal asserted.

"Whatever! It's your funeral," Drea stated, unwilling to relent her position.

"What you say?! My what?!"

"I'll call you if I think of something," Drea stated, ignoring Animal's questions before hanging up her cell phone.

"Hello!? Hello!? Drea!? Hey, Drea!?"

"You and Drea still fighting?" York asked, startling Animal so bad that he dropped his cell phone. York had been busy speaking with the surgeon who'd operated on Zahir. Animal had stood about twenty feet away from York and the doctor, never taking his eyes off the two. At least he thought he hadn't. Yet somehow, York had managed to walk up on him unnoticed.

"Nah! She's… I mean, we're good. I think my signal was cut off. But fuck that! How's my man?" Animal stated, as he bent over to pick up the dropped cell phone.

"Doctors say the surgery was a success. They expect Zahir to make a full recovery," York replied.

"So, when can we talk to him?" Animal asked.

"Doctor said he doubts Zahir will wake up tonight and suggested that any visitors should come visit Zahir sometime tomorrow evening," York replied, as he and Animal walked toward the elevators.

"Does Raquel know about Zahir's improvement?"

"Nah! She's not here," York answered Animal, as the elevator opened.

"But I thought she was watching over Zahir?"

"She is. But I told her to get Mag, so they can take turns watching Zahir. Be easy, fam. Zahir's in good hands," York replied, as he and Animal rode the elevator down.

"So, God willing, come tomorrow, Zahir should be able to tell us what he remembers?" Animal asked, pretending to be truly concerned.

"I sure as hell hope so. Look, Animal, not trying to be rude, but my stomach's smacking my back," York stated, as the elevator doors swung open.

"Mines is too," Animal stated, as both men pulled out their car keys.

"I'm going home to eat and get ready for my meeting with Sunami. If anything new comes your way concerning this, let me know," York stated.

"Alright," Animal agreed, as he dapped York, and the two parted ways. Once inside his cream-colored BMW, a new wave of overwhelming tension assaulted Animal. *Fuck! Why did Zahir have to spot me? This shit was supposed to be easy. I can't let Zahir tell what he knows. But how can I stop him? I gotta get to Zahir. I gotta silence Zahir*, Animal thought, as he cranked up his Caddy and exited the hospital parking lot.

Chapter 7

As soon as York arrived home, he called Sunami and Raquel and told them to come to his place immediately. York had a hunch. As he drove home from the hospital, York had pondered over everything that had occurred. And as hard as he tried to ignore the facts, he just couldn't. In some way, shape, form, or fashion, whether directly or indirectly, Animal had something to do with Zahir's shooting. Before calling Sunami and Raquel, York had called the captain in Zahir's crew to see if he knew why Zahir went to Rockefeller Center that morning. But Salaam, Zahir's captain, didn't have answers. Only questions. York then called Pam, who was at Zahir's home with Erin. And through Pam, he asked Erin if she knew the reason for Zahir being at Rockefeller Plaza. But once again, no answers. Just more questions. York, feeling flustered, decided to take a shower before Sunami and Raquel arrived. And while doing so, it was there, under the hot, relaxing water from the shower head, that York truly began to consider Animal as a suspect. "Why did Animal change the information Daytona had originally given him?" York contemplated, as he once again tried to explain away his doubts concerning Animal's actions. But he couldn't. Animal didn't have the ability or patience to manipulate or outthink an enemy. He was more of an all guns blazing, act now, think later type. "What the fuck is Animal up to?" York mumbled to himself, as the sound of his doorbell invaded his thoughts. After quickly drying off and throwing on one of his velvet house robes, York dashed toward the front door.

"Umm-umm! Sexy!" Raquel commented, causing York to stop mid-stride and turn toward his living room.

"If you two need some privacy…"

"I see you two have made yourself at home," York stated, cutting off the Sunami jibe.

"So, what's so important that you had us rush over here? You got the nigga who ordered the hit?"

"Where's Animal?" Raquel cut off Sunami's questions with an inquiry of her own.

"Do y'all trust me? I mean, really trust me?" York asked his two guests. "Animal's not here because I've got reason to believe he may be behind Zahir getting shot."

"What?!" Sunami stated, cutting off York's accusation.

York responded by running down the full details of the day and how Daytona swore that the information Animal had given to York hadn't come from him. The three of them sat in silence for a few moments after York completed his narration of the day's events.

"It's fucked up. But it makes sense," Raquel stated, breaking the silence.

"And how's that?" Sunami replied, as he refused to believe one of his own could have done this.

"Sunami, I know it's hard to believe, but nothing else adds up," York replied.

"I told you something wasn't right with that story. In order for Zahir to get popped like that, it had to be someone he didn't fear letting get close."

"Someone like Animal," York stated, cutting into Raquel's ranting theory.

"Naw! We fam and all, but Zahir and Animal ain't never clicked. There's no way Animal could have gotten close enough," Raquel added.

"I'll be damned!" Sunami stated then slumped into the cushion of the leather sofa.

"What is it?" Raquel asked.

"Animal might have had problems getting close enough. But Drea... Drea wouldn't," Sunami answered then looked at York.

"What?! Drea?! Shit! You ain't said nothing. I've been wanting to touch that bitch up..." Raquel said, as she pulled out her .9mm and checked its chamber for a shell. *Click-Click!*

"Be easy, love. I got a plan. Sunami, you continue enjoying your retirement. By tomorrow morning, around 9 a.m., I'll have this shit settled," York stated to Sunami then turned to face Raquel.

"And as for you, I need you to take care of the following..." York said, as he continued to instruct Raquel on his plan to set up Animal and Drea for a trap the two would find too alluring to escape.

"So, what's the hold up? Why not set the shit in motion now?" Raquel asked after hearing the plan.

"There's some loose ends I need to tie up. Just locate Drea and shadow her every move. Raquel, when you get that bitch in your sights, don't lose her. Cause when the time comes to put it down, Animal gone reach out for Drea."

"I understand," Raquel said, acknowledging York's final instructions.

After saying their goodbyes, York escorted Raquel and Sunami out of his home.

"It's time to get gully," York stated to himself, as he walked into the middle of his kitchen. York walked over to the kitchen sink and gripped the cold water knob. York pushed down on the knob then turned it backwards until the knob popped off. Under the knob was a rust proof steel button. Once pressed, the button would open a trap door York had built into the kitchen hardwood floor. *Click* was the only sound heard as the trap door opened at York's command. Inside the door was a spacious compartment that held everything from cash to passports to guns. But York paid these items no mind. All York wanted was his black duffle bag. Everything he would need would be inside that bag. "Animal, for your sake, I hope my hunch is wrong," York said to himself, as he retrieved the duffle bag and closed the trap door.

Half an hour later, York had dressed, contacted Pam, so she wouldn't stress, and was busy loading the duffle into the trunk of his tar black Bentley Continental GT when his cell phone began to ring. "Talk to me," York stated, as he answered the cell.

"Animal just arrived home. Drea was at the door when he entered. You want me to shadow him or keep tailing his bitch?" Raquel asked, seeking instruction on how to proceed.

"Stick with the bitch. If Animal is responsible for this move, you can best believe Drea's knee deep into it as well…"

"If?! What you mean if?!" Raquel asked, cutting off York's statement.

"Be easy, fam! Once I look into this loose end, I should know exactly how big a part Animal played in this bullshit," York replied.

"Hmph! You sure that's what you're doing?" Raquel asked skeptically.

"Raquel, I want Animal's ass just as bad as you do. But we owe it to Zahir to make sure we catch everyone involved with his shooting before we make any kind of move. So, keep your eyes on Drea and let me handle the rest," York declared then hung up his celly before Raquel could respond.

"I know he didn't! Girl, let that shit go. He's just stressed out." Raquel tried to reason with herself to help calm her nerves. Raquel sat half a block from Animal's crib in her midnight gray Porsche 911, awaiting Drea's next move.

As she sat doing surveillance, Raquel's mind began to recall how she first met York and how he'd introduced her to the Wolfpack Cartel. Raquel had been three weeks shy of her sixteenth birthday when she'd finally succeeded in gaining

York's attention. York was ten years her senior and had never shown any interest in her until the day she offered to help York resolve an issue. York had one of his dope spots run-in by some Jamaicans out of Brooklyn. But by sheer coincidence, one of the Jamaicans responsible for the move had a baby mother that stayed in Hammels – in the same building as Raquel and her mother, in fact. Raquel offered to handle the move but only under one condition. York, not taking the girl seriously, agreed to give Raquel whatever she wanted. Raquel could still remember the way York was laughing at her, as she left the stoop to handle her business. Raquel was a petite woman, but at almost sixteen, she was downright puny. So, she fully understood why York had taken her for a joke. But three and a half hours later when Raquel knocked on York's door with half his stolen dope and cash, she alone was laughing.

"Girl, how did you..."

"I kept my word. You gone keep yours?" Raquel asked York, as she closed his front door behind her.

"Alright, shorty. What you want?"

"Are we alone?" Raquel asked York, as the anticipation of what she was about to request caused her pulse to thump frantically.

"Uhhh... yeah!" York replied, a bit skeptically.

"Then, I want you... I want you to... to fuck me," Raquel stumbled out the words. York had stood stock-still, shocked by her request. Raquel was puny, but she had a nice figure for her size. But Raquel was extremely young. Anticipating his possible rejection, Raquel decided to put all her chips on the table.

"I'm poor, my mom's a fiend, and I got a little sister to look out for. So, spare me the 'I'm too young' speech. You got shit on smash around Queens. And I'm just trying to be down..."

"But you didn't ask me to put you on. You asked me to fuck you," York stated, cutting Raquel's speech short.

"Look, I'm a virgin. And I just spent the last three and a half hours wondering if I was gonna live or die. I swore that if I pulled this move off, I would ask you to... you know..."

"But why me?" York asked, seeking to urge her to open up more.

"If you want me to beg then just say so. Bottom line, I want to be down with you. All the way down with you. I believe that if I do right by you," Raquel stated, as she slid out her shoes and unfastened her jeans, *"that you'll do right by me. But we can talk about this later. Right now, my pussy feel funny!"* Raquel stated, as she pulled off her top.

"Alright!" York stated, as he took Raquel by the hand and led her to his bedroom.

Raquel's legs tightened, as she recalled the moments of sheer pain she suffered when York initially slid his dick into her. But her pussy began to throb, as she recalled the pleasure his dick had also provided. York spent most of that night and the following day sliding dick into Raquel, and except for the initial fucking, she'd loved every minute of it.

When York finally stopped fucking her, he never ever fucked her again. But Raquel couldn't trip because York, true to his word, had given her a spot on his team. By the time she turned eighteen, Raquel had slung dope, muled dope, pistol whipped rivals, stomped out scandalous hoes, robbed spots, and shot more than her share of niggas who'd gotten outta pocket. So, when York finally introduced her to Sunami during her birthday party, Raquel knew she'd finally been accepted. That night, Sunami asked her to join the family. And without hesitation, his invitation was accepted.

Raquel was thrust back to reality when her eyes noticed a bunch of movement. During her little flashback, Animal and Drea had managed to walk onto their front stoop without Raquel noticing. But the two hadn't made it any farther. This was due to the heated discussion the two were currently engulfed in.

"I'm stupid?! I'm stupid?! If not for you, I wouldn't be in this fucked up position. But yeah! You right. I'm stupid. Stupid for listening to your crazy ass!" Animal yelled at Drea, who stood mere inches from his face.

"Just like a bitch! Shit get a little hot, now you ready to fold! You…" Drea's venomous words were cut short, as Animal wrapped his hands around her neck.

"Shut the fuck up! You understand me?! Shut the fuck up!" Animal stated, as the grip around Drea's neck tightened.

Drea kicked and squirmed to get free to no avail. When her eyes grew heavy and began to roll into the back of her head, Animal let her loose and flung her to the ground.

"Bitch, you better be glad I need you right now. Cause if I didn't… Look… do as I told you. And all this kill York talk… dead it! Alright?!" Animal growled at Drea.

Still holding her neck and gasping for air, Drea managed to nod her head, acknowledging Animal's command. Without another word uttered, Animal left the stoop and dashed to his BMW.

"Damn! What's really going on?!" Raquel said to herself, as she watched Animal peel off, as Drea scrambled back into the house.

Chapter 8

Meanwhile, over in the Bronx, loose ends were being tied. Daytona had given York the name and address of a lady named Natalia. She was supposed to be the wifey of Hammer, the dead leader of the crew responsible for shooting Zahir.

"So, what's the problem?" Natalia asked, as York pushed his way into her apartment.

"Is anyone else in the crib?" York asked, as he scanned his surroundings. Natalia wanted to lie but decided against that when she saw York reach into his coat.

"N-No... York, I ain't never done nothing to cross you. Whatever Hammer was into ain't got shit to do with me, York. I ain't trying to die, especially not behind no bullshit!"

"Be easy! I just want to ask you some questions. Is that alright?" York stated, seeking to calm the girl before she began to cry.

"Yeah! Of course. Anything you want to know," Natalia replied, relieved to know York meant her no harm.

York drew his hand from his coat and in it he held $1,000 dollars. "You see this? It's a thousand dollars. If you tell me everything you know about today's shooting, this money is yours. All I want to know is why Hammer and his crew shot my man," York stated, as he sat on the sofa next to Natalia and placed the stack on the table in front of them.

Natalia was a cutie with ass, thighs, and legs for days. Her hair was done up in long cornrowed braids that stopped at the middle of her back. Natalia was busy twirling one around her finger, as she thought hard about what info she knew that might interest York. "Until I heard the news, I didn't know who Hammer and them was going to shoot. Honest, York! I-I don't…"

"Be easy. I believe you." York cut off her pleas with words to soothe and coax her to continue with her story.

"All I know is some guy named Beast or Monster came by here last night promising Hammer and them he'd make them part of the cartel if they shot someone for him," Natalia confessed then burst into sobbing tears.

"Calm down. I told you I wouldn't hurt you. Now, please calm down. I got one more question to ask you. Okay?!"

"Okay," Natalie answered York after regaining her composure.

"Are you sure the guy was named Beast?" York asked, prying for more info.

"Beast. Monster. I'm not sure. But I know it was some kinda…"

"Animal?" York threw out the name to see how she'd react.

"Yeah! Yeah! That's it. I knew it was something along that line. You know him?" Natalia asked, as York sprang up from the couch.

"We never had this conversion. Understand?" York stated, as he turned to leave her crib.

Natalia sat stock-still, as she watched York close the door behind him as he left. "Animal, Beast, whatever your name is, I feel for you. I feel for you," Natalia said to herself, as she leaned forward and grabbed the stack of cash.

***

While York was receiving confirmation on Animal's involvement in Zahir's shooting, Animal was busy visiting an unlicensed doctor with a specialty in providing customers with any drug they desired. If you had the cash, Dr. Stiller had the drug.

"Voilà! What you see in this vial is my infamous cocktail from hell," Dr. Stiller stated, as he gave Animal the vial.

"Don't bullshit me, Doc. Does this shit really work?" Animal asked, as he examined the vial.

"If you follow my instructions to the letter, my cocktail will handle the rest," Dr. Stiller assured Animal.

"So, all I gotta do is mix this cocktail with four spoonfuls of water then put it in a syringe and inject it into my tiger," Animal asked, restating the instructions.

"Sir, if you own a tiger, then my name is President Bush. Listen, Sonny, whatever or whoever you use that cocktail on will be shaking hands with Jesus shortly after. And that's a promise," Dr. Stiller affirmed, as he escorted Animal out the front door of his establishment.

You better be right, Doc. Cause I swear I'm not ready to meet Christ, Animal thought to himself, as he pocketed the vial and approached his BMW.

***

The sun was beginning to set, and Raquel was becoming restless, as she continued to stake out the home of Animal and Drea. "Come on, bitch, do something," Raquel murmured to herself, as she scanned through the stations on her phone. "Oh, hell yeah! That's my shit!" Raquel proclaimed, as the Mobb Deep classic *Shook Ones* began to play. "Damn! The last time I heard this was…" Raquel began to say, as her mind lost itself to the beat and journey down memory lane once more.

The Wolfpack Cartel had shown the streets who was really running shit in N.Y. But to do this meant going to war with one of the already established thoroughbreds. And during the early 90s, there were a shitload of them to choose from which made Sunami's task of selecting which crew to attack all the more difficult. That was until the day Shadow got stomped out and shot up by Jamaicans out of Brooklyn. Once Sunami heard this, the choice became simple. The Jamaican crew was led by a Rasta who called himself General. He called his crew the Jamrock Clan, and they were treacherous. The only reason Shadow had escaped the assault with his life was due to the fact that the Jamrock Clan actually believed they had killed him. That was the first of two costly mistakes the clan would make. Their second mistake was doubting the heart of the Wolfpack Cartel. It had taken three days for Sunami to come up with the plan for revenge, but his plan was perfect. At that time, the Wolfpack Cartel only had two wolves. That was Zahir and Animal.

Sunami and York were boss and consigliere, while Raquel, Lord, Shadow, Salaam, and Mag were cartel captains. Everyone else was viewed as cartel members. Sunami decided to assemble two three man teams, one led by him, the other by York. The plan was to coax General and his top two men, Paul and Ben, out their homes. All three of them stayed in a housing unit on Hancock Street with their families. Sunami and his team's job was to create the chaos needed to bait out the three men. And with General's true weakness being his love for family, Sunami knew just how to draw him and his top dogs out. Sunami's team consisted of Animal, Shadow, Lord, and Mag, leaving York in charge of Zahir, Raquel, and Salaam. Sunami gave Mag and Lord two AKs and four full clips and ordered them to shoot-up the Jamrock Clan's biggest dope spot. Sunami and Animal had the easiest task of all. Their job was to terrorize General's little brother, a Rasta named Dawu.

Dawu lived a square life, and due to that fact, he never saw what was coming until it was too late. Sunami and Animal kicked in the door to Dawu's home that morning and caught Dawu, his wife, and daughter eating their breakfast. Animal wasted no time letting his .357 talk to Dawu, as he whipped Dawu viciously with the butt of his pistol.

"Unless you want your wife and kid to feel it, you better call your brother and tell him this," Sunami said to Dawu, as he passed Dawu a message to read to his brother.

Dawu gave no resistance to Sunami's demand and did exactly as he was told.

Sunami had Dawu call General and tell him that his family had been kidnaped.

"What?!"

"Brethren, they got me family. Get here with $150,000 in four hours or me and family dead Ya hear! Dead!" Dawu said to General, as he conveyed Sunami's written message word for word.

"Simmah down, brethren. Me on the way," General stated then slammed the phone onto the floor.

"What's wrong, me love?" asked Zina, General's wife.

"No-ting, me love. No worry for me love," General replied, as he quickly dressed himself.

As General scrambled to get ready, Sunami and Animal were busy laying down phase two of their mission.

"Tie up these motherfuckers," Sunami ordered Animal, as he grabbed his cell phone and paged York to signal his team to get ready.

Beep-Beep-Beep! York's pager went off, signaling his team into action.

"Alright, fam! That's our cue. As soon as General and his boys exit the building, let them have it," York ordered his team.

"I wish these niggas would hurry up. These fucking fishnets are killing me," Raquel stated, as she tucked her .357 into the small of her back and covered it with her coat.

"Everybody knows their jobs, right?!" York asked.

"Yeah, son, We got this," Zahir replied, as he and Salaam checked the chambers of their AKs then exited the rear of the car.

"Remember, when I honk my horn..."

"Yo, York! We got it!" Zahir affirmed, as he and Salaam each folded a cardboard box around their AKs to conceal them.

"And as for you, you sure you wanna do this?" York asked Raquel, who sat next to him in the front of the car.

"I don't see why not. The hard part's already done," Raquel replied.

"And what was that?"

"Putting on this fucking slut suit!" Raquel replied, as she hopped out the front of the car and strolled off down the block to get into position.

Zahir was leaning on the corner of the building that General and his top two men would exit, while Salaam sat on the bottom step of the building's stoop, pretending to be drunk. Raquel strolled the sidewalk across the street from General's home, and though she hated to admit it, she actually pulled off the slut role rather well. Just as Raquel caught her stride good, York honked the horn and cued the attack. General had burst out the front door of the building, carrying a Desert Eagle in his right hand and a bookbag in his left. On General's heels were his top two clansmen, Paul and Ben. The trio had reached the second step of the stoop before they stopped to acknowledge the sound of York's blowing horn. As soon as General and his two top dogs turned their heads up the block toward York's direction, Zahir and Salaam removed the cardboard from their AKs and started tattooing the stoop with steel. Salaam set the trio ablaze from the front, while Zahir stood to the left of the trio, spitting flames. General, Paul, and Ben weren't given enough time to cry out for Jah (God), as death snatched their lives instantaneously.

"Alright, baby girl! Come do your thang," Zahir screamed over his shoulders to Raquel, as he and Salaam watched the building, looking for any type of movement.

Raquel dashed up the stoop to do what York considered necessary. *Boom-Boom-Boom-Boom!"* Raquel stood over *each man and shot them once in the head, except for General. She shot him twice. York didn't want some miracle to pop off where, somehow, one of the three Rastas survived the AKs. So, Raquel's job was to put a bullet in each of their heads to ensure this didn't happen.*

Rat-Ta-Tat-Tat'

"Move! Move! I saw movement upstairs!" Zahir yelled, as he and Salaam let their AKs remodel the face of the building.

Raquel bent over and untied the bookbag from General's dead hands then sprinted off the stoop.

Screetch!

"Hop in!" York yelled toward Raquel as he screeched his car to a halt in front of the building. Honk-Honk-Honk! "Zahir! Salaam! Come on! Let's go!" York shouted.

Raquel rolled down the front passenger side window to provide them with cover, and once Zahir and Salaam were secure in the backseat, York sped off. Moments later, Sunami's cell phone rang.

"Alright! Meet you at the spot in twenty minutes," Sunami stated then hung up his celly. Now, it was time to leave a lasting message for the rest of the Jamrock Clan. "Animal, go start the car. I got this," Sunami stated, as he tossed the keys to the whip.

As soon as Animal exited the crib, Sunami walked over toward the living room where Dawu, his wife, and toddler daughter were sitting duct taped up. Sunami drew his snub nosed .38 and aimed it at the wife.

"Mmph! Mmph!" Dawu tried to speak, but his mouth had been duct taped. Boom-Boom! Two bullets ripped apart the head and chest of Dawu's wife. Boom-Boom! Without hesitation, Sunami put matching holes into Dawu, leaving him with only the toddler to kill.

Boom! Sunami's last shot found its home into the base of the living room wall. I'm not killing no kid, Sunami thought, as he placed his gun into his rear pocket and took off out the crib.

"Yep! That was the last time I heard that song," Raquel stated, as the song *Shook Ones* began to go off, and her trip down memory lane ended.

Suddenly, Raquel's eyes caught movement on the stoop of Animal and Drea's crib. It was Drea, and she was carrying her two kids to the car. Drea placed her one-year-old daughter in a car seat on the rear seat of the champagne-colored Benz Jeep. Then, she buckled up her three-year-old son next to the baby. Drea shut the door to the Benz then nervously scanned up and down the block, as she dashed back into her home. Moments later, Drea exited the home pulling five suitcases on a trolly.

Looks like somebody's trying to get low, Raquel thought to herself, as she watched Drea load the luggage into the back of the Benz. Once the luggage was stored, Drea climbed behind the wheel of the Benz and pulled off, ignorant to the fact that she was being followed.

Chapter 9

Meanwhile, at a Starbucks in Times Square, York sat in a corner booth nursing a cappuccino and scheming on the best way to lure and trap Animal and Drea. York had tried calling Animal and Drea directly, but neither of them were answering their cells. *I should have kept you close,* York mentally stated to himself in regard to allowing Animal the freedom to roam. But with Mag watching over Zahir at the hospital and Raquel shadowing Drea, York was confident that one of the two would spot Animal. York had just gotten off the phone with Mag and had ordered Mag to call him if Animal showed up at the hospital. So, with all his bases covered, the only thing York had left to do was scheme and plot on how to trap Animal.

***

Back in the Bronx, Raquel's job of tailing Drea had taken an interesting twist. Instead of driving to some out-of-town hotel or distant relative's home, as Raquel had assumed Drea was doing, Drea was instead creeping down Hunts Pointe, looking at prostitutes. "What the... This shit ain't making no sense," Raquel murmured to herself, as she watched Drea's Benz Jeep come to a halt.

"Excuse me! You with the blonde hair. Come here please," Drea yelled out the driver's window of the Jeep. The prostitute Drea called for was standing with three more call girls, but she was the only snow bunny in the bunch.

"Ah, you talking to me?" the white prostitute asked Drea, a bit skeptical.

Drea, being in no mood to talk, flashed a thick wad of cash at the pink toe and motioned for the prostitute to come closer. "You want to make some serious money?" Drea asked the whore.

"Are you police?" the whore replied, ignoring Drea's question and instead posing one of her own.

"What's your name, baby?" Drea asked the whore, as she flashed the cash once more for the slut.

"Umm… Wendy. You can call me Wendy," the whore replied.

"I want you to look over my shoulder, Wendy," Drea said, as she leaned sideways to allow Wendy to easily view her two sleeping kids.

"Oohhh! They so pretty," Wendy cooed out her praise.

"Yes, they are. Now tell me, Wendy, how many cops roll like this?" Drea asked, motioning toward her kids.

"None I know," Wendy replied, as she began to flirt with Drea with her eyes.

"Hop in. Let's talk business, baby," Drea instructed Wendy who, without further hesitation, obliged.

"What the fuck?!" Raquel stated, completely befuddled by the scene she'd just witnessed.

As soon as Wendy entered the car, Drea pulled off. And just as before, Raquel was hot on her tail.

***

"What's up?!" Salaam said, as he answered his phone.

"Yo, Salaam, it's me," York stated.

"What's the word?" Salaam asked, seeking to know if any new news had surfaced concerning Zahir's shooting.

"We'll discuss that later. Right now, I need you to suit up," York replied.

"York! What's going on?" Salaam asked.

"Like I said, now's not the time. I need you to suit up, and while you're at it, scoop Lord, Lamel, and Life and head over to Mt. Sinai," York ordered.

"You want them to suit up too?" Salaam asked.

"Yeah! Now, once you get to the hospital, I want y'all to go to the cafeteria and wait for Raquel to show. Once she get there, she'll tell y'all what to do from there," York instructed him.

"Alright! We'll be there within the hour," Salaam replied.

"Salaam! Do you know how to get the guns past security?" York asked him.

"I'll figure out something," Salaam replied.

"Listen up. This is what you do…" York stated, as he began to instruct Salaam on how to bypass the hospital metal detectors.

***

Raquel again was thrown for a loop, as Drea made yet another unpredictable move. Once more, Raquel had figured that Drea's next, most logical stop would have been a hotel room. But this was not the case.

"You strap down the kids… load up a trunkful of luggage," Raquel contemplated over the actions she was witnessing, as she continued shadowing Drea, "then pick up a trick… and now here you go pulling into the parking lot of the Cedar Hurst Hospital? What the fuck are you up to, bitch?" Raquel pondered, as she watched Drea hop out the Benz Jeep and sprint into the main entrance of the hospital. Raquel's mind was working triple time trying to process Drea's actions, but nothing she came up with made any sense.

As Raquel began to consider a new array of possibilities, Drea dashed back out the hospital with what looked like hospital scrubs in her left hand and a bag in her right hand. "Now, why would you need hospital scrubs? This bitch must really be into role playing… or… Umm-hmm! Now that makes sense," Raquel mumbled to herself, as she reached for her cell phone and called York.

***

Meanwhile, over at Mt. Sinai hospital, the hit squad was busy getting into position. Salaam had entered the hospital to look for an empty room. He lucked up and found one on the second floor overlooking the same parking lot his team was loitering in. "Heey, yooo!" Salaam yelled out from the second-floor window. Lord, Lamel, and Life stood only a few feet away and dashed over to stand under the window Salaam leaned out of. "Lord, catch the line. Lamel! Life! Y'all cover him," Salaam said, as he dropped down one end of the rope.

Once the rope reached Lord, he quickly went to work. Lord opened up his coat and pulled out a black medium sized trash bag. The bag contained five .9 mms and five extra clips. Lord took the rope and tied it around the knot that kept the bag closed Once this was done, Lord, Lamel, and Life walked away from the spot and headed for the hospital cafeteria. Salaam waited for the trio to get a safe distance away then scanned the parking lot to ensure he wasn't being watched. Once he was certain that no one was looking, Salaam pulled the bag. After securing the window, Salaam quickly opened the bag and stashed the weapons all over his body. With the task complete, Salaam made his way toward the cafeteria to join the others.

***

"A trick... and hospital scrubs?"

"Yep! I think they gone use the scrubs to get close to Zahir. I just can't figure out the purpose of the trick," Raquel replied to York, as she continued to shadow Drea while conversing with him on her celly.

"You sure she hasn't spotted you?" York asked.

"I don't think so," Raquel answered.

Beep-Beep!

"Hold on, shorty!" York said to Raquel, as he clicked over to see who was on his other line. "Talk to me," York said, as he answered the other line.

"What's the word?" Animal asked York.

"What's the word?! Nigga, where the fuck you've been?" York barked the words out.

"At one of my shorty's crib, getting my eat on. What I..."

"Your celly broke?! Cause I been calling you for the last two hours," York stated, as he interrupted Animal.

"York, I accidently left my cell in the car. What's going on?" Animal nervously asked, praying like hell that York hadn't found out about his shady actions.

"Salaam and his crew got clapped at by some of Chase's crew. Look, I ain't got time to get into all the details. Call Raquel and she'll tell you what I need for you to do. Alright?" York replied.

"Yeah, I'm on it," Animal answered.

"Animal! Call-her-now!" York ordered Animal then hung up before he could reply.

"York?!"

"Yeah, I'm back! Look, Animal's about to call you. You know what to do?" York asked Raquel when he clicked back over to her line.

"Yeah!" Raquel answered.

"When he calls, put it in motion," York instructed Raquel.

"Alright! But what about Salaam and his crew?" Raquel asked.

"They already at the hospital, waiting on you," York replied.

"Oh, shit!" Raquel blurted out.

"What's wrong?" York asked but received no immediate response.

Raquel had gotten so caught up in talking with York that she'd almost crashed into the back of the car she was using as a shield to shadow Drea. Drea was two car lengths ahead, parallel parking her Jeep, and her attempts had caused traffic on the street to halt.

"Yo, Raquel! What's going on?" York yelled out, trying to receive a reply.

"Drea's parking," Raquel answered, as she scanned the block for a parking space, but instead of spotting a parking space, she spotted Animal. Animal was walking off the porch of the home Drea was attempting to park in front of.

"You not gone believe this," Raquel said to York, as she threw her Porsche's gear into reverse.

"What's up?" York asked.

"I've got Animal in my sights. That's what's up. So, what you wanna do?" Raquel asked, hoping York would let her off the chain.

"I want you to write down the address. Park the car and peep the spot out as best as you can from within your car. If Animal calls you, give him the bait then go to the hospital. But if he doesn't call, stay put and keep shadowing him and Drea. I'll cover the hospital if you gotta deep shadow," York explained to Raquel, who agreed to follow his orders and hung up.

York knew Raquel was mad. He knew she wanted to end shit then and there. But unlike York, Raquel couldn't see the bigger picture. With Zahir well protected, and with Animal and Drea both under watch, there was no way for Animal to hurt Zahir. But there were many ways for York to hurt Animal. York couldn't afford to let this incident pass, not without using it as an example to the rest of the cartel of what could happen when certain lines were crossed. York's hospital trap was nothing more than his way of testing how far Animal would go to silence Zahir. To York, the killing of Animal and Drea was already a for gone conclusion. The only matter still left to decide was in which way they'd be killed.

***

"It's about fucking time!" Animal stated to Drea, as he opened the rear door and began unbuckling the kids.

"You act like you surprised or something. You know I can't parallel park," Drea replied, as she hopped out the Benz and circled around the SUV to grab her kids.

"Have you told her what's up?" Animal asked Drea, as he handed her their baby girl.

"Her name's Wendy and no! I ain't told her shit. It's your plan, so you tell her," Drea said defiantly then turned her back to Animal and headed up the stairs to enter the house.

Animal swallowed his tongue and took a deep breath, attempting to cool off. "If we make it out of this shit alive, I'm gonna break that bitch neck," Animal swore to himself, as he rounded the SUV and entered the driver's side. "Alright, Wendy! I need you to listen carefully. I ain't got time for games. I need you to answer my questions with yes or no answers. Understand?" Animal lit into Wendy as soon as he closed the car door.

"Ahh, I mean yes!" Wendy replied a bit nervously.

Animal pulled out and counted five thousand dollars then placed the money in her hand.

"I just placed five thousand dollars in your hand, and all you got to do to keep that money is do everything I ask you to do tonight. Now, what I need to know right now is if you have a problem with following that one simple rule?" Animal asked, as he leaned over toward Wendy and placed his left hand on her thigh.

"Uh-uh... I mean, no. I ain't got no problems with that," Wendy replied.

"Good! Now, let's discuss..." Animal paused mid-sentence, as he slid his hands up Wendy's thigh. Wendy took a deep breath and opened her legs wider to give Animal easier access. "Let's discuss what I expect," Animal finished his sentence, the tip of his index finger brushing against Wendy's damp cunt.

"Oo-ah!" Wendy gasped out in a mixture of pleasure and shock. Animal leaned closer to Wendy then took his right hand and unbuckled her seatbelt.

After releasing the seatbelt, Animal took his right hand and removed Wendy's hair from her left ear. Wendy's pulse was jumping all over the place. She was nervous yet excited. Aroused yet a bit frightened. Animal's fingers continued to gently stroke in and out of Wendy's cunt, driving her crazy. As a prostitute, her pussy, ass, or mouth always had something probing them. But not like this. Wendy couldn't remember the last time anyone had touched her tenderly.

Oh, shit! He's licking my ear. That's my spot. That's my motherfucking spot! Wendy mentally proclaimed, as her back arched, and her clit swelled with arousal.

With the doors locked and with the Benz windows laced with mirror tint, Animal was free to do as he pleased with Wendy with no fear of being seen. *Damn, she wet!* Animal thought, as he slid a fourth finger into her cunt without ever breaking the slow, gentle rhythm. "You're so fucking hot! So incredibly hot!" Animal whispered in Wendy's ear then arched her head back and began to suck on her neck.

"Oohhouu, shit!" Wendy moaned out, as Animal's finger fucking and neck sucking demolished her senses.

"Make love to my hand, baby! I want you to..." Animal once again paused mid-sentence, but this time, he started gently rubbing his thumb over Wendy's clit with the same rhythm he stroked her pussy with. And once Wendy's body locked up as he'd expected it would, Animal put on the most sincere expression he could manage and looked Wendy square and deeply in the eyes and finished his sentence. "Make love to my... yes! Ohh! Yes! That's it," Animal tenderly stated, as Wendy began to slow wind all over his fingers. Wendy was consumed with emotions, and none of them were good. At least not for a woman in her profession.

How did this happen? Wendy thought momentarily before Animal's sweet words and gentle fingers stroked her into an even deeper emotion submission. It was like watching a ton of bricks crumble into dust. As Wendy's body completely fell under Animal's lustful spell, Wendy's physical submission was complete. And this was signified by the tear that slowly trickled from her eye.

"Talk to me, baby. Speak to me, baby," Animal gently said, as he continued to softly stroke her cunt toward a second orgasm.

"I'm yours, baby. I'm yours!" Wendy moaned out the words that came not from her mouth but her soul.

"Yes, baby! Yes, you are," Animal soothingly replied, as he reclined and slid back the front passenger seat to its max to prepare Wendy for her mental raping. Animal climbed over the passenger side of the Benz Jeep and positioned himself between Wendy's legs. He took his hands and placed them each on the opposite sides of Wendy's headrest.

"I can hold you... I can kiss you from head to toe... I can please you with my tongue... or with my dick. I can do oh so many things to you, but none of these things ae what I truly want," Animal said to Wendy, as he stared lovingly down into her eyes. "What I want is to make you feel like a woman, not some whore," Animal said to Wendy, as he stared lovingly down into her eyes, "but a truly adored woman. But I can't give you this gift unless you allow me. Wendy, I need you to surrender completely to me. Allow me to touch the real you. Open yourself completely to me. Not just your body. No, baby. I want your soul," Animal stated then leaned down and kissed Wendy. His kiss was deep and lovingly tender. Wendy initially hesitated, but just as her body had moments before, her mind too surrendered to Animal's seduction. Once Animal broke the kiss, he knew he had her.

Now, I must conquer the fear caused by her submission, Animal mentally noted, as he gazed into her eyes and noticed the fright within them. "What's wrong, baby? You look so scared," Animal asked, as he stared lovingly once more into her face.

Wendy was a natural blonde with piercing, deep blue eyes. She had what some would call a California tan which made her skin a beautiful, sun kissed brown. As far as Animal could see, she had no needle marks or any other signs upon her that would indicate that she'd done drugs. Wendy looked to be around nineteen or twenty-one. Give or take. And from what Animal could see, Wendy was holding in all the right places. Wendy's breasts were full C-cups that naturally stood at attention, her thighs and calves were thick and toned, and her hips were thick enough for Animal to assume that she was packing ass as well. Her face wasn't stunning or even beautiful, but it was cute. Animal hovered about Wendy, silently admiring her, as he gave her time to build up her courage to voice her fears. "What happens after… after tonight?" Wendy whispered out her question.

"Tonight becomes tomorrow. Then tomorrow becomes a week…" Animal began his answer.

"Are you a pimp? Just be real with me. It'll save you a lot of time if you just let me know. I've had one before, nothing like you of course, but he… you know… he…" Wendy stated before fumbling over how to describe her introduction to prostitution.

"He introduced you to prostitution," Animal finished the sentence for her.

"Well, if you call slapping and kicking an introduction, then that's what I got," Wendy stated, seeking to bring some humor to a bleak topic.

"Wendy," Animal called her name and took his right hand and caressed her face. "I'm no pimp. And what I'm offering you is the return of your dignity – a dignity no one can snatch from you unless you let them. I wanna make you mine, Wendy. And I... I want you to make me yours," Animal said, laying it all on the line.

"But what about your family?" Wendy asked, referring to Drea and the babies.

"Drea?! That's my sister. You mean... you thought... Ha-ha-ha-ha!" Animal burst into laughter to sell his lie even more, and Wendy, like all star gazers, took the bait and fell for the lie.

"I just... you know..."

"Shh!" Animal silenced her rambling by gently placing his index finger over her lips. "Wendy, I asked you to let me give you a special gift. A gift to renew your womanhood. A gift that will be yours for as long as you desire it. I stand before you symbolizing that gift. Are you..."

"Shh!" Wendy silenced Animal by taking her right hand and covering his mouth, and with her left hand, she unzipped his jeans and pulled out his cock. Once his dick sprang free, Wendy cupped his balls with her right hand and gently stroked his cock in an up and down motion with her left one. "I don't know how to be a woman..." Wendy spoke while her eyes were staring down at Animal's dick. The shame of her confession weighed down her neck, keeping her from looking into Animal's face.

"Are you willing to learn?" Animal asked her, as he tilted her head up, so he could stare into her face.

"Yes! I'll do whatever you need me to do. Anything!" Wendy replied.

"Right now, all I want you to do is claim your gift," Animal stated. He took his right hand and ran it through her hair.

"I can do that!" Wendy proclaimed with a smile then opened her mouth to suck his cock. But right before her lips touched his pole, Animal gently pushed her away from his dick.

"Uh-uh, baby. Tonight... this nigh... I make you a woman," Animal stated, as he lay Wendy flat against the seat and lifted her hips for better access.

Wendy bit her bottom lip and looked at Animal with an expression of shock and pleasure. Animal unfasted his jeans and let them fall to his ankles, while Wendy spread her legs as wide as she could to accommodate him.

Time to close the deal, Animal said to himself, as he shifted between Wendy's thighs and slowly fed dick to her pussy.

***

Meanwhile, at the Starbucks café, York was still awaiting Raquel's call. "What the hell is taking her so long?" York contemplated over why Raquel hadn't called him back. York's mind was so consumed by thoughts that he never saw Sunami enter the Starbucks café. It was only when Sunami began to sit in the chair across from him that York noticed him. "What you... how'd you know I was here?" York asked.

"Let's just say me and the manager are... good friends," Sunami replied, as he pointed to an attractive woman behind a nearby counter to show York who he was referring to.

"Hmm! Friends my ass! So, what's up? I know you didn't come out here to check on me!" York stated, as he picked up his cup of cappuccino and played with it.

"Me check up on you?! Nah! But... I do think we need to talk," Sunami replied.

"Sunami, I already told you I got this," York said, as he placed his cup onto the counter.

"I'm sure you do, but you still gone listen to what I've got to say," Sunami stated, as his face became stern.

"Look, fam, I'm not trying to blow you off, but can we do this another time?" York asked, as he pulled out his celly and toyed with it.

"If it could wait, I wouldn't be here. Now listen..." Sunami stated, as York exhaled loudly. "You remember our battle with the Jamrock Clan?" Sunami asked.

"Yeah! That battle is what put us on the map," York answered.

"Well, ever since that day, I've been haunted by this one question."

"Yo, fam, it was either them or us. Ain't shit to be haunted over," York said, cutting off Sunami.

"You're right. And if everyone did as they were supposed to that day..."

"Hold up! What are you trying to say? Everyone executed their jobs perfectly," York asserted, as he once more cut off Sunami.

"I didn't. I made a decision that's been haunting me ever since," Sunami confessed.

"What you saying, Sunami?" York asked.

"Dawu had a little girl..."

"That you killed. I know all this." York finished his statement for him.

'No, York. I didn't kill her. I couldn't. And if you'll shut up long enough to let me talk, I 'll explain why this decision haunts me," Sunami stated.

"I'm listening," York said then wrapped his hands around his coffee cup.

"Nothing in the streets stays a secret for long. Eventually, with enough time, even our best buried secrets become revealed. York, I'm not saying my choice to let that girl live was wrong. But what I will say is that because of that choice, I've spent the last five or so years watching my back. Wondering if this will be the day that little girl catches up with me. I don't know her name. I don't have a clue on how she even looks, but what I do know is that the streets know and are going to tell that little girl who killed her parents. Maybe she already knows my name. Maybe she's in this café, watching me right now…"

"So, what you saying, Sun? I know you ain't here copping pleas for Animal," York interjected.

"Bruh, if I didn't love you, I'd leap cross this table and choke the shit out of you. Listen, nigga, and listen good! I don't care how you handle Animal or his bitch. I'm just trying to keep you from making the same mistake I made. Bottom line is on one day, I didn't do what I probably should have, and because of that mistake, I will spend the rest of my days looking over my shoulders."

"Sun, just spit it out. Cause on the real, you got my wires all crossed the fuck up," York stated, seeking some clarity.

"All I'm saying is, whatever you decide to do concerning Animal… do it! Don't leave nothing to chance, York. Go all out, fam. Cause if you don't… Well, if you don't, you'll spend the rest of your days watching your back too," Sunami warned York, who got ready to reply, but the ringing of his celly stopped him.

"Talk to me," York said into his celly, as Sunami rose up from the table.

"I just got off the phone with Animal," Raquel replied.

"Hold on… Where you going?" York asked Sunami, as he covered the celly with his free hand.

"I've done what I came to do. Now, if you don't mind, I've got a retirement present to collect," Sunami stated then walked toward the nearby counter and began chatting with the lovely café manager.

"York! Yo, York!" Raquel shouted through the celly, seeking to get a response.

"Yeah, what's up? Did he take the bait?" York asked.

"Did he! I thought the nigga was gonna leap through the phone and kiss a bitch!" Raquel answered.

"So, now you're a bitch?!" York coyly asked.

"Normally, *no*! But tonight, you can best believe I'm gone be the Queen Bitch!' Raquel replied.

"You still shadowing…"

"Nope! I'm on my way to the hospital," Raquel replied, cutting off York's question.

"Good. Call me when you've caught the rats," York stated.

"Hold up! Wait a minute! You ain't coming to the hospital?" Raquel asked, shocked that York wasn't joining in on the action.

"Nope. I've got to go secure Plan B," York replied.

"Plan B?" Raquel asked, clearly confused.

"I'm going to stake out the house you followed Drea to. I want to make sure that if the rats somehow manage to escape your trap that they fall from one trap directly into another," York answered.

"That's what's up," Raquel stated.

"I thought you might like that… bitch!" York said, saying the last work playfully before he hung up his celly.

"Time to set up shop," York said to himself, as he rose from the table, waved bye to Sunami, and exited the café.

***

Back over in the Bronx, plans of a different kind were being finalized. "I don't like this plan," Drea said, as she lay her baby girl on top of a blanket on the floor.

"Hmph! I wonder why," Animal snidely replied.

"You know what… Fuck you, nigga! If you wanna run off and get yourself killed… then go! But I won't be with you!" Drea spazzed, as she circled around the couch to avoid being within Animal's reach.

"Bitch, you think I need you to pull this off?! Bitch, please! Me and shorty got this!" Animal replied angrily.

"Shorty?! Who? That whore in the back?! Nigga, please! You tripping!" Drea stated then started to chuckle.

110

"Drea, you can laugh all you want. Say whatever you want. It don't matter. You not gone piss me off. Not tonight," Animal replied, as he picked up his coat and prepared to leave.

"Is that's what you think? That I'm trying to piss you off? Then you dumber than I thought. Animal, the shit too easy. It's gotta be a trap," Drea argued.

"Okay! Uh, yeah!" Animal replied with blatant sarcasm.

'Oh, so now I'm crazy! If you go to that hospital, it's your…"

"How do I look? Oh, I'm sorry. Am I interrupting?" Wendy said, as she walked into the living room, interrupting Drea's rant.

"No, you're not interrupting. Damn, you wearing the hell outta them scrubs," Animal stated, as he motioned for Wendy to join him at the door.

"Thank you. I do try," Wendy playfully said, seeking to lighten the dark mood invading the room.

"After you, Ms. Doctor," Animal playfully replied, as he opened the door for them to exit.

"Animal, I'm not through with you," Drea said, as Wendy exited the home.

"Your mom will be home soon. Talk to her cause you and me… We's through!" Animal replied with such conviction that he robbed Drea of any ability to respond. As soon as the door closed behind Animal, Drea crumbled to the floor in tears.

They gone kill my baby! God, please don't let them kill my baby, Drea silently pleased, as her sobs grew stronger.

***

Meanwhile, back in the hospital cafeteria, a meeting was coming together as planned.

"It's about damn time," Life said, as Raquel reached their table.

"I'm gone act like I didn't hear that. Now, slide your rude ass over," Raquel replied, as she shoved Life to help him move over faster.

"What the hell is going on, Raquel?" Salaam asked as soon as she was seated.

"We know who shot Zahir."

"Who?!"

"Animal," Raquel replied

"What?! Say word," Salaam stated, as he and the other three men at the table were stunned by the news.

"Look, I don't have the time to get into all the details. We've got a trap to set. And speaking of which, I believe you have something for me," Raquel stated.

"Life's got it," Salaam answered, cueing Life to hand Raquel a gun and a spare clip.

Raquel shielded the weapon with her body and the table. Then, she checked the chamber and both clips to ensure all was good. "Alright! Now, let's get down to business. We don't have much time..." Raquel stated, as she paused mid-sentence to tuck the 9mm into the small of her back. "In the next ten to fifteen minutes, Animal's gone stroll into this hospital to finish off Zahir. And we're gonna let him stroll all the way into Zahir room..."

"What?!" Lord and Lamel said, cutting off Raquel.

"Salaam! Check your niggas," Raquel stated then resumed disclosing the plan after Salaam ice grilled his crew back into silence.

Lamel, Life, and Lord were nothing more than hired guns. The cartel paid them a salary and regarded them as family. But being told the ins and outs of the inner workings or operations of the cartel was knowledge not made privy to them. Whenever Lord, Life, and Lamel were called for business, it was only for one reason. And that was to put in work. Salaam was Zahir's captain and was in charge of the cartel's hit squad. Salaam was no slouch when it came to gun play either which was why no one, especially not Life, Lord, or Lamel, objected to Salaam heading the hit squad. As soon as Salaam had gotten the call, he knew what it was. *I never liked the nigga anyway*, Salaam thought to himself then focused back to the conversation at hand.

"It's as simple as that. My job's to catch him trying to kill Zahir. And you and the squad's job is to make sure Animal don't escape once the trap is set," Raquel instructed, as she rose from the table to leave.

"Does York want this nigga taken alive?"

"Dead! When you get my call, that's the signal to let him feel it," Raquel stated, cutting off Salaam's question.

"Everyone check your chirps," Salaam said, as he and everyone at the table began checking their throw away celly to ensure everything was good to go.

"Everybody good?" Raquel asked, as she pocketed her celly.

"Yeah!" they all replied.

"Alright. Lamel, you watch the elevators. Lord, you watch the east stairwell, while Life watches the west stairwell. I want y'all to chill on the first floor of the stairwells in case he comes down your way. If that happens, move in for the kill. Alright?" Raquel asked to ensure everything was clear.

"Yeah!" the trio answered.

"And you, I need you to man the front entrance. I don't' see how he could possibly reach the front entrance once the trap is sprung. But if by chance he does…"

"I'll peel his fucking balls!" Salaam stated, as he cut off Raquel, letting her know he more than understood the score.

'That's what's up," Raquel said then turned and walked out the cafeteria to head upstairs.

***

"You back?! I thought York said Animal was coming to relieve me?" Mag asked Raquel, as she approached where he sat in front of Zahir's room.

"He is. I'm only here to look in on Zahir once more for Erin. The girl won't rest unless someone did. How about you? You good?" Raquel asked, as she stood over Mag's sitting frame.

"I need to take a fucking piss. But other than that, I'm good," Mag replied.

"Then go piss. I'll look in on Zahir. Just be back before Animal arrives. Lord knows if that fool gets here and don't see you."

"I know. Trust me, I know. He gone flip," Mag stated, cutting Raquel's comments off, as he rose from his chair and headed for the restroom.

Raquel wasted no time entering Zahir's room. Once inside, Raquel paused momentarily to look at Zahir. "Fight, baby! You just keep fighting," Raquel murmured the words then crossed the room to set up shop. The room held two beds. Each bed was positioned on opposite sides of the room, facing each other.

"Salaam, is everything good on your end?" Raquel hit Salaam on her celly, as she drew back the draw curtain to give her a full view of Zahir's side of the room.

"Everybody is set. You good?" Salaam answered back, as Raquel cut off the room lights.

"I'm set," Raquel replied, as she kneeled down and began to slide herself behind the headboard of the empty hospital bed.

***

"Wendy, are you sure you can do this? If you walk into that room and get cold feet..."

"Animal, will you relax please? My pimp had me doing shit far more worse than this," Wendy stated, cutting off Animal's comments, as she reassured him that she was fine.

"Wendy, just humor me. Let me hear you say that you're sure you can do this," Animal said, as he pulled out the syringe containing the cocktail.

"I'll do even better than that. Give me that needle, and I'll show you how sure I am," Wendy said, as she retrieved the syringe from Animal and pocketed it into the doctor's coat she wore.

"Well, since you put it like that, let's go," Animal said, as he led Wendy away from his parked SUV and toward the main entrance of the hospital.

"Raquel, get ready. Animal just walked in," Salaam phoned Raquel with his warning.

"Was Drea with him?" Raquel asked.

"No, but he wasn't exactly alone either," Salaam replied. That was when everything Raquel had seen while shadowing Drea finally fell into place.

"Let me guess... blonde head white girl in hospital clothes," Raquel described.

"Uh, yeah! How'd you..."

"Later. I'll tell you later," Raquel said then hung up her celly.

As soon as Raquel hung up her celly, Animal and Wendy were exiting the elevator on Zahir's floor.

"I know; I know. You gone have some guy with you. Don't say nothing to you. Just walk around the corner, go up the hall, and enter the fourth room on the right," Wendy stated, letting Animal know she knew the score.

Animal said nothing more. He simply nodded his head in approval and turned and walked around the corner of the hall that led to Zahir's room. Wendy shifted her weight from foot to foot, as she awaited the appearance of Animal. Even though she knew it wasn't possible, Wendy swore that the syringe was burning a hole in her pocket.

It's a woman beater... He's gone hurt Animal. He deserves this. Wendy mentally ran over all the excuses Animal had given her for killing Zahir, as she awaited Animal's arrival. "Fuck! What's taking so long?" Wendy worried, as she crept toward the corner to sneak a peek up the hall. But as soon as she was about to peek, she heard Animal's voice.

"So, if I need you to come back later on tonight, you could do it?"

"Yeah! If you need me, just call," Mag answered Animal's question, as the two men entered Wendy's line of sight.

And like a bullet, Wendy was off. She briskly walked up the hall and wasted no time dipping into Zahir's room. *Hmph! Oh, you're Zahir. I thought you'd be bigger,* Wendy thought to herself, as she stood by the door, surveying the room.

Come on, pink toe. Show me your back, Raquel silently requested, as she watched Wendy retrieve the syringe from her pocket. Wendy pulled the protective cap from the syringe and dropped it back into her pocket. As soon as Wendy circled the foot of Zahir's bed, Raquel quietly slid out from behind the opposite bed's headboard. Wendy wasted no time and neither did Raquel.

Chapter 10

As soon as Wendy slid the needle into Zahir's I.V., cold steel slapped her skull. "Ungh!" Wendy yelped, as she staggered into the nearby corner, attempting to avoid further assault.

"Bitch, shut the fuck up!" Raquel said, as she aimed her 9mm at Wendy's face.

Raquel glanced over at the I.V. and noticed the syringe was still lodged within it. "Did you shoot any of that shit in him?" Raquel asked, as she snatched Wendy by her shirt and pointed the 9mm between her eyes.

"No!" Wendy answered.

"Good! Now pull that syringe out and recap it," Raquel ordered Wendy, who tentatively complied. Once this was done, Raquel made Wendy repocket the syringe. "Now, if you want to live, you'll do exactly as I say. Understand?" Raquel said to Wendy, as she took two steps away from her and retrieved her celly with her loose hand. "I'm only gonna say this to you once. You lie and I'll throw your ass headfirst out that muthafucking window. Understand?" Raquel stated. Wendy nodded her head to show she understood. "Where is Animal?" Raquel asked.

"He told me to meet him at the main entrance... when I... when I..."

"Say it and I'll shoot your dumb ass right now!" Raquel said, as she phoned Salaam. "Salaam, he's coming your way. Tell everyone to converge on your spot," Raquel ordered.

"Alright!" Salaam replied.

'Now, as for you, we gone walk out of here, side by side, talking like two long lost friends. You break fool, and I'll pump your ass drunk," Raquel said to Wendy, as she flung the phone into her left coat pocket. "Let's go!" Raquel ordered, as she shifted to place Wendy on her left side and led her out the hospital room.

"Man, fuck that! Soon as that clown step out the elevator, I'm pulling the rachet," Lamel said to himself, as he disregarded Salaam's order and continued to await the electors. *Ding! Ding! Ding!* Three of the four elevators flung open simultaneously. "Shit!" Lamel said, as he reached for his piece, without drawing it, and dashed from elevator to elevator looking for Animal.

Each elevator was packed due to the changing of shifts by the hospital staff. It was while Lamel was looking through the second elevator that Animal and Mag slid out the third.

"Yo, son, ain't that Lamel?" Mag asked Animal, as he pointed Lamel out to Animal. Animal didn't reply because as soon as he looked where Mag was pointing, Lamel had spotted them and was making his way toward them.

Fuck! I been setup! Animal mentally concluded, as that and a hundred other thoughts raced through his mind.

"Yo, Mag, move, son!" Lamel ordered, as he pulled out the 9mm and aimed for Animal, who stood behind Mag.

"Oh, God! Help!" a bystander shouted, as they noticed the gun brandished by Lamel.

Soon, the surrounding onlookers were screaming and scrambling for cover.

"Yo, yo, son! What the fuck is this?!" Mag asked, trying to figure out why Lamel had whipped out on them.

"Mag! Get the fuck out the way," Lamel growled out the words, as two nearby bystanders dashed into the elevators just rear of Animal.

Animal caught sight of this and realized that without a gun, his only real option was to run. And the elevator was his best option. Mag had just begun to slide out of Lamel's way when Animal grabbed Mag by his shoulders and flung him at Lamel. The elevator doors were in the process of closing, as Animal leaped inside and scrambled to the side for cover.

"Fuck!" Lamel screamed, as he reached the elevator too late to get off the shot.

"Lamel, what the fuck is going on?" Mag asked, at a complete loss.

"Fuck! I gotta get this nigga," Lamel stated, as he ignored Mag and sprinted for the east stairwell.

As Lamel ran for the stairs, Lord and Life appeared on the scene. "Lamel! Yo, Lamel!" Lord screamed out at Lamel, but he ignored Lord's call as well then dipped up into the stairwell.

"Hold up! What the fuck is going on?" Mag asked angrily.

"Chill, fam! Yo, Life, go catch that nigga," Lord ordered then pulled out his phone.

"Chill! Man, fuck that! I wanna know…"

"Yo, Salaam, we got problems. I think Animal spotted Lamel," Lord said, as he phoned Salaam.

"What?! Fuck! Where's he at now?" Salaam asked.

"I don't know where Animal's at…"

"He jumped back in the elevator when Lamel pulled on him," Mag said, interrupting Lord.

"Yo, Mag said Animal took the elevator back up when Lamel drew his piece," Lord relayed Mag's statement.

"Where's Lamel?" Salaam asked.

"He ran up the east stairwell. I guess he…"

"You and Mag take the west stairwell. You take the first floor, tell Mag to cover the second," Salaam ordered.

"Come on, son!" Lord said to Mag, as he sprinted toward the west stairwell.

"Yo, Raquel!" Salaam phoned her to tell her about the situation.

"You got him?" Raquel asked, as she and Wendy rode down the elevator.

"Nah! He spotted Lamel and dipped back upstairs."

"What? Fuck! So, where is he now?" Raquel tersely asked.

"I'm not sure. Lamel is in direct pursuit of him. But I've got Lord and Mag covering the west stairs while Life covers the east. Raquel, trust me, we gone get this nigga," Salaam stated.

I can't believe this shit, Raquel thought to herself. "Salaam! I'm coming your way," Raquel stated then closed her celly, as she and Wendy rode down the elevator toward Salaam.

Looking for a way out of the hospital, Animal had hopped off the elevator on the floor above the main entrance and was franticly looking from left to right for a means of refuge. *I gotta lay low… need somewhere to hide,* Animal thought to himself, as he quickly darted down the first hall he saw. Animal went from room to room, looking for an empty one, but each time he opened a door, someone was inside. It was as Animal closed the door to another occupied room that Lord spotted him.

"Yo, Salaam! I found him. He's on the floor above you," Lord relayed the message and dashed up the hall after him. But when Lord's celly chirped off, Animal heard the beep and turned to peep what it was.

"Fuck!" Animal cursed, as he spotted Lord closing in on him. Animal opened the next door on his right and darted inside. The room was occupied by a patient and nurse, but Animal paid them no mind. as he ran to the room's window and looked out of it. "I can make it," Animal concluded, as he assessed the distance of the drop. Animal tried to open the window, but it wasn't built for opening.

"Sir, can I help you?" the female nurse asked, visibly bothered by Animal's presence.

"Yeah, stay the fuck out of my way!" Animal said, as he backed away from the window as far as he could.

"Oh, dear! He's gonna jump!" the lady patient exclaimed, as Animal took off running full speed toward the window. Animal leaped, shoulders first through the window, and no sooner than he broke the window did Lord burst through the door.

"Fuck!" Lord yelled out, as he ran over toward the busted window. Animal was dashing across the parking lot by the time Lord spotted him.

"Yo, Salaam! Parking lot! He's in the parking lot." Lord phoned Salaam with the news.

"Shit!" Salaam cursed, as he turned and sprinted out the main lobby toward the main entrance. But it was too late. By the time Salaam exited the hospital, Animal's SUV was peeling out of the parking lot.

"Fuck! Fuck... Fuck... Fuck!" Salaam cursed, as he watched Animal escape.

"He... two stories up... He just..."

"Round up the squad and follow me. I've got a good idea where he's heading," Raquel said, cutting off Salaam's frustrated ranting.

"Lord! Phone the squad and tell them they got two minutes to get to the car," Salaam relayed Raquel's order.

"Come on, bitch!" Raquel said to Wendy, as she nudged her through her coat with the gun and led her toward her Porsche.

Chapter 11

"Many men, many, many, many men… wish death upon me…" The words of 50 Cent's song, *Many Men*, flowed through the speakers of York's Bentley Continental GT, serving as mood music for York, as he opened his black duffle bag and strapped up for war. The sun had long ago set, and the block was relatively empty, all of which were to York's advantage. York parked under a broken streetlight a block over from the home Raquel had given him directions to.

York took off his black leather coat and strapped on his bulletproof vest. Then, he threw on his twin shoulder holsters and slid a .45 into each of its sleeves. After doing this, York retrieved two silencers from his bag and deposited them into the pocket of his leather coat. "Go all out… or spent the rest of your days looking over your shoulders." Sunami's words of warning crossed York's mind, as he slid back into his leather coat.

"Hmph! Won't be no watching over my shoulder. Not if I can help it," York swore to himself, as he placed on a pair of leather gloves and exited the car.

York walked over and stood directly under the same broken streetlight he was parked up under. *Perfect,* York thought to himself, as he looked up and down both sides of the block he stood upon.

The block had cars parked in almost every available spot, and every house on the block had hedge bushes that could offer York the perfect cover if he crouched low.

Yep! Absolutely perfect, York mentally concluded once more, as he pulled out his celly and called Raquel. Raquel was about five minutes away from the spot when she received York's call.

"What's up?" Raquel said, as she answered her celly.

"Where you at?" York asked.

"I'm sitting at a stop light about five minutes away. Has he shown up yet?" Raquel asked, as she glanced over at the passenger floorboard of her Porsche to check on Wendy.

Raquel had made Wendy sit upside down within the car with her head on the floorboard and her feet on the seat. This allowed Raquel to drive without having to worry about Wendy trying anything slick.

"Nah, not yet! Look, I want Salaam to watch the side of the house. The rest of the squad hold down the front," York stated, as he watched the headlights of a SUV turn down the block.

"What about me? Let me do that bitch, York. You gotta…"

"Hey, hey, hey! As soon as you get here, come inside the house," York stated then hung up his celly. "Time to rock," York mumbled to himself, as he watched the SUV begin to park in front of the house he'd been staking out.

Animal had finally arrived, but due to his own haste to park, Animal paid no attention to the block. Animal mistakenly still believed he was one step ahead of the cartel.

"Run in… get the kids… Drea… then hit the highway," Animal mumbled to himself, as he hopped out the Benz Jeep and headed for the house.

Thump! Pain raced through Animal's left calf as a .45 slug ripped through his flesh, causing him to stagger and fall to the ground.

"Fuck!" Animal cursed, as the reality that he'd been shot began to set in. Animal began to reach for his waist to pull his 9mm, but the sensation of hot metal against his temple made him freeze in his tracks.

"I'm only gonna ask you once. Stand up!" York ordered Animal, who complied.

"Yo-York?! What's going on?" Animal pretended to truly be confused.

"We'll talk inside," York replied, as he motioned for Animal to approach the house.

Animal complied once more but only after York gripped the back of his neck and pinned the gun to the back of his spine.

Inside the home, Drea was pacing around the living room, worrying herself to death about Animal. Drea's son lay asleep on the couch, while Drea's mom, who'd arrived home an hour earlier, was fussing.

"If my man had choked me, the last thing I'd be worried over is when he's coming home," said Ms. Roberta, Drea's mom.

"How many times I gotta tell you? He didn't choke me. At least not in the way you're thinking," Drea replied, as she checked her watch for the millionth time.

"You can talk to you turn blue in the face. And I'm still not gone believe you got that bruise around your neck from having rough sex. Hmph! Rough sex my ass," Ms. Roberta stated.

"Mom, I'm really not..." Drea's retort was cut short by the sound of the front door opening. "Animal! Boy, I was worried sick about you. So, what happened... Oh, shit!" Drea rambled then cursed aloud when she spotted York standing behind Animal.

"Get on your knees and hold out your hands," York commanded Animal, as he removed the .45 from his spine and aimed it at Drea's head.

"Oh, my God!" Ms. Roberta yelped, as she identified the cause of her daughter's distress.

"God ain't got shit to do with this. Put the kid down and step behind Drea," York ordered Ms. Roberta.

Ms. Roberta placed the baby on the couch next to her sleeping brother.

"Now, look, son..."

"Step behind the bitch!" York restated his command to Ms. Roberta, cutting off her attempt to speak. But Ms. Roberta chose to ignore York's command once more and attempted yet again to reason with York.

"If you'll only..."

Thump-Thump!

"Aahhh!" Drea screamed hysterically, as two slugs ripped through Ms. Roberta's chest.

"I'm only gone say shit once," York said, as he backed up to the front door and pushed it until it nearly closed.

"Ahhh! My mom! You killed... Momma!" Drea continued to scream and cry.

"Bitch, shut that shit up before I put matching holes in your kids!" York's threat instantly silenced Drea.

"Will someone please tell me what the fuck is going on?!" Animal yelled out, still pretending to be clueless about the cause for York's actions. But instead of fooling York, Animal only managed to awaken both the kids.

"Oh, so now you wanna act like a bitch!" York growled out the word, as he smacked the back of Animal's dome three times with the .45, but in the process of pistol-whipping Animal, he took his eyes off Drea.

Drea wasted no time. She grabbed a nearby eight-inch porcelain statuette of Jesus and smacked York viciously across the side of the head. If her blow would have landed full flush, York would've hit the floor. Instead, her blow landed half flush, causing York to stumble forward.

What the fuck?! York thought momentarily, as he tried to regain his balance.

Drea spun to grab another porcelain statuette, as Animal realized what had happened and reached for his gun. By the time Drea prepared to strike York again, he'd shook off the blow.

Thump-Thump!

Bang! All three shots popped off simultaneously, but only one hit flesh. York's second shot hit Drea in the right shoulder, spinning her body left. Animal, still groggy from the pistol whipping, just missed hitting York by a few inches. York shoved Drea to the floor of the home's hallway, as he dove behind the front of the couch for cover.

***

Meanwhile, in front of the house, Raquel and the hit squad were parking their cars. "What the fuck?!" Raquel stated, as she heard the gunshot Animal had fired. "Bitch, get the fuck out!" Raquel ordered Wendy, as she snatched Wendy by her hair and dragged her from the passenger, seat to the driver's side, then out the car.

"You heard that, right?" Salaam asked Raquel, as she continued to drag Wendy up the sidewalk.

"Just get everybody into position. I'll handle the rest," Raquel stated then commenced to dragging Wendy's ass up the steps to the house.

Back inside the house, things were becoming very interesting. "I didn't want to kill you, York. All I want to do is get out of here with my life," Animal stated, as he struggled to get to his feet, but York wasn't trying to talk. He was scanning his brain for a way to get back on top of the situation. His options were limited. The couch blocked him from knowing exactly where Animal was crouching. So, he couldn't shoot at him either. And that was when it hit him. The perfect way to get back on top of things. Drea was too far to get at, but her kids weren't. "So, what's it gonna be, York?" Animal asked, as he finally managed to get to his feet.

"I don't know, nigga! You tell me!" York said, as he stood up, dangling the toddler in front of him as cover.

"No, please! Not my baby," Drea pleaded, as she watched York dangle her son upside down by his ankles.

Fuck! Animal thought, as he realized that though he had a gun, he now, more than ever, was still at York's mercy. Animal was so preoccupied by the scene before him that he never noticed Raquel enter the home.

Pop! Pop! Pop! Pop! Raquel let loose four shots, all of which found homes within Animal's flesh. One hit him in his shoulder, causing him to twist away from Raquel, as the last three shots lodged into his lower back and butt cheek.

"Aahhh! Fuck!" Animal screamed, as he crashed back down onto the floor.

"Please... York, please don't kill my baby." Drea continued to plead for York to spare her child. Raquel had pressed Wendy against a side wall when she'd first entered the home, and as Drea pleaded, Raquel flung Wendy over toward York.

"I caught this bitch trying to poison Zahir," Raquel stated, as she walked over on top of Animal and kicked the gun out of his hand.

"So, why ain't she dead?" York asked. But Raquel didn't respond – at least not with words anyway.

Raquel let off a shot that tore a hole clean through Wendy's skull. She was dead before she hit the floor. Brain matter from Wendy's skull splattered onto York's face, causing him to drop the toddler on his head, breaking his neck.

"Nooooo! You sick motherfucker! I'm gonna..."

Pop-Pop!

Raquel fired two shots that tore through Drea's chest. Drea's body, which had been jolting toward York, was flung backwards by the shots. Drea hit the floor, took two gasps for air, then joined her mother in death.

"She dead?" York asked, as he circled the couch to stand over Animal and Drea's slumping bodies.

"Yeah, she dead," Raquel replied, as she kicked Drea in the pussy to prove her point.

"Good. Now take care of that baby," York ordered then crouched down toward Animal's slumping frame.

"You want me to kill a baby?!" Raquel asked.

"Kill it. Keep it. I don't care what you do with that lil motherfucker!" York stated, as he lifted Animal's head and made him look at his face.

Animal knew it was useless to beg for his life. He also knew that he didn't want to die. The combination of these two profound emotions caused Animal to shed tears profusely.

"It didn't have to be like this," York stated then placed the .45 against Animal's chest.

"Tell me, York... tell me who..." Animal's request could have been referring to almost anything, but York knew the caliber of man Animal was and knew that even facing death, remorse was the farthest thing from Animal's heart. Animal's lust for power had led him to death's door, and his thirst for it, even when facing death, still couldn't be quenched. So, when Animal asked York to, 'tell him who...', he knew exactly what Animal was asking about.

"It was you, Animal. The cartel's next boss would've been you," York answered him.

The look on Animal's face was one of pure anguish, and from deep within him, York took extreme pleasure from Animal's pain. And without another word spoken, York pumped two .45 slugs point blank range into Animal's heart then dropped his head back to the floor.

"Raquel! Let's go!" York stated, as he stood up and looked around for Raquel. But the room was empty except for the dead body that lay at his feet and those around the room. York stood alone...

Epilogue

Mt. Sinai Hospital

Erin's high heeled stilettos and her occasional mumblings were the only noises being made outside of Zahir's hospital room. The two uniformed cops, compliments of the N.Y.P.D., had learned the hard way to leave Erin alone. The guard's attempt to console her had resulted in a full-on verbal assault that could've made the devil himself cower.

Erin hadn't slept since discovering Zahir had been shot and had spent the past night pacing the floors worrying and awaiting any type of coherent movement from Zahir.

"Oh, my God!" Hypnotic exclaimed, as she looked upon the nervous wreck that was Erin. Hypnotic and Pam had come along with their mates to check up on Zahir. All stood in awe, looking at the pacing hot mess that was Erin.

"Pam take Hypnotic and go get Erin to eat something," Sunami stated, as he slapped York with the newspaper, attempting to silence his snickers.

"Don't hit me! Hit her! Maybe then she'll take her butt home and wash," York replied jestingly.

"Kill the jokes, York! The woman is grieving," Sunami stated, as Hypnotic and Pam escorted Erin toward the elevator, a feat that, in itself, was no easy task. "Look at these clowns! I wonder if they know they're protecting a gangster?" York said, as Sunami began pulling out his wallet. The police guards had been given a short list of names authorized to visit Zahir. Each visitor had to present a valid ID before being admitted inside Zahir's room.

"I'll vouch for this one, fellas," Nurse Burrell stated, as she re-opened the room's door and signaled for Sunami and York to enter. "Zahir's vitals are growing stronger. He was just awake, but he's still heavily sedated, so don't expect him to do anything more than ramble."

"Thanks for the…" York began his reply but was cut short by the nurse's comments to the boys in blue. "Now, which of you fine, uniformed men is gonna join me for breakfast?" Nurse Burrell asked then rubbed the cop to her right, as Sunami pulled York into the room.

The room was dimly lit by the rays of the morning sun that shone through the room's lone window. An array of beeps, clicks, and what sounded like compressed air filled the room with noise, but the sight of Zahir looking like a science project gone bad left both Sunami and York speechless.

Damn, Zay! Keep fighting, fam, Sunami exclaimed mentally, as he viewed Zahir's ghastly pale body.

What the… These fools gots my man looking like a Black Frankenstein, York stated mentally, as he tried to no avail to count the number of tubes entering and exiting Zahir's body.

"Looking at Zay… looking like this… makes me wonder why I took so long to retire," Sunami said, as he tapped York's chest with the newspaper.

"I feel you, but don't fret for Zay. He'll pull through," York stated, as he took the newspaper from Sunami's hands and watched him cross the room and take a seat.

"But what about you? How you holding up?" Sunami asked, as York took a seat in the chair next to him.

"I'm good. See!" York replied, as he held up and presented the front page of the metro section for Sunami to view.

"I'm not talking about your Bronx fiasco. How you doing?"

"I'm good. But I'll be much better when Zay takes over. With you out, there's no need for me to stay in," York answered, as he took a long glance out the room's window.

"And what will you do if Zahir wishes to retire? Near death experiences tend to alter a man's priorities at the very least," Sunami said, seeking to provide York with a little food for thought.

"If that's how it goes, then Raquel will have to step up."

"Are you sure about that? Because I heard she was getting her parenthood on," Sunami ruefully retorted.

York looked long and hand at Sunami and wondered which member of the hit squad had seen Raquel leave with the baby. "So, you know about that? What else did you hear?"

"That's not important. But what is important is that you stabilize the business and restore order within the family. Do this and I'll do more than just attend your retirement party. I'll host it," Sunami stated then turned his face and looked out the window.

"I don't think so. I do all that, and I will, you gone do more than just host. You gone foot the bill, negro!" York declared, causing Sunami to chuckle.

"Yor… Ahh! York!" Zahir called out to York in a ghastly, raspy whisper.

"Zahir! We're here, fam!"

"That's my motherfucking, man. How you feeling, fam?" York exclaimed following Sunami's announcement.

"York… I… I was…" *Cough-Cough!* "Ohh!" Zahir tried to speak.

"Be easy. Relax, fam," Sunami said.

"This should help you relax better," York added, as he held up the headline page of the metro section for Zahir to read. The headline read: Five People Found Dead. Zahir looked from the newspaper back to York's face with a look of utter confusion written over his face. "Read this paragraph… right here," York said, as he pointed to the paragraph of interest. It read: "The bodies of five people were discovered in a Bronx home late last night. Police say they received an anonymous call and were told they would discover dead bodies inside the home. Among the discovered was the body…" Zahir read each name of the dead bodies recovered from inside the home. Two names in particular instantly illuminated Zahir's drear face. A look of peace began to enfold Zahir, as he realized that York and the cartel had already handled the traitorous culprits responsible for his shooting. "That's right, fam. You can relax. We handled that scummy ass…"

"York! Bugs work in hospital rooms too!" Sunami interjected, cutting York's discourse short.

"Umm!" Zahir peacefully moaned, as he allowed himself to drift back off to sleep.

"That's it. Get your rest, Zay. You've got a cartel to head," York stated in a low murmur to himself. Then, he walked away from the bed and reclaimed his seat by the window. Both men briefly looked upon each other with a certain quiet satisfaction. Then, each man reclined in their seats and once again glanced out the room's lone window.

To Be Continued...

Lock Down Publications and Ca$h Presents Assisted Publishing Packages

Due to an increase in the price of services we have increased our prices. The prices below reflect the price increase as of 11/1/24.

BASIC PACKAGE	UPGRADED PACKAGE
$699	**$1000**
Editing	Typing
Cover Design	Editing
Formatting	Cover Design
	Formatting
	Upload eBooks to Amazon
	Upload Paperback to Amazon
ADVANCE PACKAGE	**LDP SUPREME PACKAGE**
$1,400	**$1,700**
Typing	Typing
Editing (line editing/content)	Editing (line editing/content)
Cover Design	Cover Design
Formatting	Formatting
Copyright Registration	Copyright Registration
Proofreading	Proofreading
Upload eBooks to Amazon	Set up Amazon Account
Upload Paperback to Amazon	Upload eBooks to Amazon
	Upload Paperback to Amazon
	Advertise on LDP's Amazon and Facebook Page

***

Other services available upon request.
Additional charges may apply

Lock Down Publications
P.O. Box 944
Stockbridge, GA 30281-9998
Phone: 470 303-9761
Email: lockdownpublications@gmail.com

Submission Guideline

Submit the first three chapters of your completed manuscript to ldpsubmissions@gmail.com. In the subject line add **Your Book's Title**. The manuscript must be in a Word Doc file and sent as an attachment. Document should be in Times New Roman, double spaced, and in size 12 font. Also, provide your synopsis and full contact information. If sending multiple submissions, they must each be in a separate email.

Have a story but no way to send it electronically? You can still submit to LDP/Ca$h Presents. Send in the first three chapters, written or typed, of your completed manuscript to:

LDP: Submissions Dept
P.O. Box 944
Stockbridge, GA 30281-9998

DO NOT send original manuscript. Must be a duplicate. Provide your synopsis and a cover letter containing your full contact information.

Thanks for considering LDP and Ca$h Presents.

NEW RELEASES

BLOODLINE OF A SAVAGE 1-3
THESE VICIOUS STREETS 1-3
RELENTLESS GOON 1-3
BY PRINCE A. TAUHID

THE BUTTERFLY MAFIA 1-3
BY FUMIYA PAYNE

A THUG'S STREET PRINCESS 1&2
BY MEESHA

CITY OF SMOKE 3
BY MOLOTTI

GET IT IN SLUGS 1 &2
BY B. STALL

STANDING ON HER BUSINESS 1&2
BY DG SANTANA

STEPPERS 1,2&3
THE REAL BADDIES OF CHI-RAQ
BY KING RIO

THE LANE 1&2
BY KEN-KEN SPENCE

THUG OF SPADES 1&2
LOVE IN THE TRENCHES 2
CORNER BOYS
BY COREY ROBINSON

TIL DEATH 3
BY ARYANNA

HOOD CONSIGLIERE 3 | KEESE

THE BIRTH OF A GANGSTER 4
BY DELMONT PLAYER

PRODUCT OF THE STREETS 1-3
BY DEMOND "MONEY" ANDERSON

NO TIME FOR ERROR
BY KEESE

MONEY HUNGRY DEMONS 1-2
BY TRANAY ADAMS

HUB CITY MENACE 1-3
BY J. WHITE

A THUGGISH PASSION 1&2
LAND OF DA HOOLIGANZ 1-4
KILLAZ ON STANDBY 1&2
BY IRA B.

FO'EVA ROLLIN 1&2
BY ASSA RAYMOND BAKER

THE LEVEL UP 1&3
BY LUXURY KING

Coming Soon from Lock Down Publications/Ca$h Presents

IF YOU CROSS ME ONCE 6
ANGEL V
By Anthony Fields

A THUGS STREET PRINCESS 3
By Meesha

CORNER BOYS 2
By Corey Robinson

THA TAKEOVER
By Keith Chandler

BETRAYAL OF A G 2
By Ray Vinci

SAVAGE FAMILY EMPIRE 1&2
SOULLESS GOON 1,2&3
THE DIRTY SIDE OF MONEY 1,2&3
By Prince

FOR MY ENEMY'S SAKE
AMBITIONS OF A SLIDER
FRESH OFF DA PORCH
By IRA B.

THE TRUCKLOAD 1-4
TIPPIN' THE SCALES 1-3
BAD BITCHES WIT GUNZ 3
PROBLEM SOLVED 2
By Christopher "Diesel" Hornezes

Available Now

RESTRAINING ORDER 1 & 2
By **CA$H & Coffee**

LOVE KNOWS NO BOUNDARIES 1-3
By **Coffee**

RAISED AS A GOON I, II, III & IV
BRED BY THE SLUMS I, II, III
BLAST FOR ME I & II
ROTTEN TO THE CORE I II III
A BRONX TALE I, II, III
DUFFLE BAG CARTEL I II III IV V VI
HEARTLESS GOON I II III IV V
A SAVAGE DOPEBOY I II
DRUG LORDS I II III
CUTTHROAT MAFIA I II
KING OF THE TRENCHES
By **Ghost**

LAY IT DOWN I & II
LAST OF A DYING BREED I II
BLOOD STAINS OF A SHOTTA I & II III
By **Jamaica**

LOYAL TO THE GAME I II III
LIFE OF SIN I, II III
By **TJ & Jelissa**

IF LOVING HIM IS WRONG…I & II
LOVE ME EVEN WHEN IT HURTS I II III
By **Jelissa**

PUSH IT TO THE LIMIT
By **Bre' Hayes**

HOOD CONSIGLIERE 3 | KEESE

BLOODY COMMAS I & II
SKI MASK CARTEL I, II & III
KING OF NEW YORK I II, III IV V
RISE TO POWER I II III
COKE KINGS I II III IV V
BORN HEARTLESS I II III IV
KING OF THE TRAP I II
By **T.J. Edwards**

WHEN THE STREETS CLAP BACK I & II III
THE HEART OF A SAVAGE I II III IV
MONEY MAFIA I II
LOYAL TO THE SOIL I II III
By **Jibril Williams**

A DISTINGUISHED THUG STOLE MY HEART I II & III
LOVE SHOULDN'T HURT I II III IV
RENEGADE BOYS 1-4
PAID IN KARMA 1-3
SAVAGE STORMS 1-3
AN UNFORESEEN LOVE 1-3
BABY, I'M WINTERTIME COLD 1-3
A THUG'S STREET PRINCESS 1&2
By **Meesha**

A GANGSTER'S CODE 1-3
A GANGSTER'S SYN 1-3
THE SAVAGE LIFE 1-3
CHAINED TO THE STREETS 1-3
BLOOD ON THE MONEY 1-3
A GANGSTA'S PAIN 1-3
BEAUTIFUL LIES AND UGLY TRUTHS
CHURCH IN THESE STREETS
By **J-Blunt**

CUM FOR ME 1-8
An LDP Erotica Collaboration

BLOOD OF A BOSS 1-5
SHADOWS OF THE GAME
TRAP BASTARD
By **Askari**

THE STREETS BLEED MURDER 1-3
THE HEART OF A GANGSTA 1-3
By **Jerry Jackson**

WHEN A GOOD GIRL GOES BAD
By **Adrienne**

THE COST OF LOYALTY 1-3
By **Kweli**

BRIDE OF A HUSTLA 1-3
THE FETTI GIRLS 1-3
CORRUPTED BY A GANGSTA 1-4
BLINDED BY HIS LOVE
THE PRICE YOU PAY FOR LOVE 1-3
DOPE GIRL MAGIC 1-3
By **Destiny Skai**

A KINGPIN'S AMBITION
A KINGPIN'S AMBITION II
I MURDER FOR THE DOUGH
By **Ambitious**

TRUE SAVAGE 1-7
DOPE BOY MAGIC 1-3
MIDNIGHT CARTEL 1-3
CITY OF KINGZ 1&2
NIGHTMARE ON SILENT AVE
THE PLUG OF LIL MEXICO 1&2
CLASSIC CITY
By **Chris Green**

HOOD CONSIGLIERE 3 | KEESE

A GANGSTER'S REVENGE 1-4
THE BOSS MAN'S DAUGHTERS 1-5
A SAVAGE LOVE 1&2
BAE BELONGS TO ME 1&2
A HUSTLER'S DECEIT 1-3
WHAT BAD BITCHES DO 1-3
SOUL OF A MONSTER 1-3
KILL ZONE
A DOPE BOY'S QUEEN 1-3
TIL DEATH 1-3
IMMA DIE BOUT MINE 1-6
DYING FOR LIKES
By **Aryanna**

A DOPEBOY'S PRAYER
By **Eddie "Wolf" Lee**

THE KING CARTEL 1-3
By **Frank Gresham**

THESE NIGGAS AIN'T LOYAL 1-3
By **Nikki Tee**

GANGSTA SHYT 1-3
By **CATO**

THE ULTIMATE BETRAYAL
By **Phoenix**

BOSS'N UP 1-3
By **Royal Nicole**

I LOVE YOU TO DEATH
By **Destiny J**

I RIDE FOR MY HITTA
I STILL RIDE FOR MY HITTA
By **Misty Holt**

LOVE & CHASIN' PAPER
By **Qay Crockett**

TO DIE IN VAIN
SINS OF A HUSTLA
By **ASAD**

BROOKLYN HUSTLAZ
By **Boogsy Morina**

BROOKLYN ON LOCK 1 & 2
By **Sonovia**

GANGSTA CITY
By **Teddy Duke**

A DRUG KING AND HIS DIAMOND 1-3
A DOPEMAN'S RICHES
HER MAN, MINE'S TOO 1&2
CASH MONEY HO'S
THE WIFEY I USED TO BE 1&2
PRETTY GIRLS DO NASTY THINGS
By **Nicole Goosby**

LIPSTICK KILLAH 1-3
CRIME OF PASSION 1-3
FRIEND OR FOE 1-3
By **Mimi**

TRAPHOUSE KING 1-3
KINGPIN KILLAZ 1-3
STREET KINGS 1&2
PAID IN BLOOD 1&2
CARTEL KILLAZ 1-3
DOPE GODS 1&2
By **Hood Rich**

THE STREETS ARE CALLING
By **Duquie Wilson**

STEADY MOBBN' 1-3
THE STREETS STAINED MY SOUL 1-3
By **Marcellus Allen**

WHO SHOT YA 1-3
SON OF A DOPE FIEND 1-4
HEAVEN GOT A GHETTO 1&2
SKI MASK MONEY 1&2
By **Renta**

GORILLAZ IN THE BAY 1-4
TEARS OF A GANGSTA 1/&2
3X KRAZY 1&2
STRAIGHT BEAST MODE 1&2
By **DE'KARI**

TRIGGADALE 1-3
MURDA WAS THE CASE 1-3
By **Elijah R. Freeman**

SLAUGHTER GANG 1-3
RUTHLESS HEART 1-3
By **Willie Slaughter**

GOD BLESS THE TRAPPERS 1-3
THESE SCANDALOUS STREETS 1-3
FEAR MY GANGSTA 1-5
THESE STREETS DON'T LOVE NOBODY 1-2
BURY ME A G 1-5
A GANGSTA'S EMPIRE 1-4
THE DOPEMAN'S BODYGAURD 1&2
THE REALEST KILLAZ 1-3
THE LAST OF THE OGS 1-3
By **Tranay Adams**

MARRIED TO A BOSS 1-3
By **Destiny Skai & Chris Green**

KINGZ OF THE GAME 1-7
CRIME BOSS 1-4
By **Playa Ray**

FUK SHYT
By **Blakk Diamond**

DON'T F#CK WITH MY HEART 1&2
By **Linnea**

ADDICTED TO THE DRAMA 1-3
IN THE ARM OF HIS BOSS
By **Jamila**

LOYALTY AIN'T PROMISED 1&2
By **Keith Williams**

YAYO 1-4
A SHOOTER'S AMBITION 1&2
BRED IN THE GAME
By **S. Allen**

TRAP GOD 1-3
RICH $AVAGE 1-3
MONEY IN THE GRAVE 1-3
CARTEL MONEY 1&2
By **Martell Troublesome Bolden**

FOREVER GANGSTA 1&2
GLOCKS ON SATIN SHEETS 1&2
By **Adrian Dulan**

TOE TAGZ 1-4
LEVELS TO THIS SHYT 1&2
IT'S JUST ME AND YOU
By **Ah'Million**

KINGPIN DREAMS 1-3
RAN OFF ON DA PLUG
By **Paper Boi Rari**

THE STREETS MADE ME 1-3
By **Larry D. Wright**

CONFESSIONS OF A GANGSTA 1-4
CONFESSIONS OF A JACKBOY 1-3
CONFESSIONS OF A HITMAN
CONFESSIONS OF A DOPE BOY
By **Nicholas Lock**

I'M NOTHING WITHOUT HIS LOVE
SINS OF A THUG
TO THE THUG I LOVED BEFORE
A GANGSTA SAVED XMAS
IN A HUSTLER I TRUST
By **Monet Dragun**

QUIET MONEY 1-3
THUG LIFE 1-3
EXTENDED CLIP 1&2
A GANGSTA'S PARADISE
By **Trai'Quan**

CAUGHT UP IN THE LIFE 1-3
THE STREETS NEVER LET GO 1-3
By **Robert Baptiste**

NEW TO THE GAME 1-3
MONEY, MURDER & MEMORIES 1-3
By **Malik D. Rice**

CREAM 2-3
THE STREETS WILL TALK
By **Yolanda Moore**

THE STREETS WILL NEVER CLOSE 1-3
By **K'ajji**

LIFE OF A SAVAGE 1-4
A GANGSTA'S QUR'AN 1-4
MURDA SEASON 1-3
GANGLAND CARTEL 1-3
CHI'RAQ GANGSTAS 1-4
KILLERS ON ELM STREET 1-3
JACK BOYZ N DA BRONX 1-3
A DOPEBOY'S DREAM 1-3
JACK BOYS VS DOPE BOYS 1-3
COKE GIRLZ
COKE BOYS
SOSA GANG 1&2
BRONX SAVAGES
BODYMORE KINGPINS
BLOOD OF A GOON
By **Romell Tukes**

CONCRETE KILLA 1-3
VICIOUS LOYALTY 1-3
BLOODY MONEY BAGS
By **Kingpen**

THE ULTIMATE SACRIFICE 1-6
KHADIFI
IF YOU CROSS ME ONCE 1-3
ANGEL 1-4
IN THE BLINK OF AN EYE
By **Anthony Fields**

THE LIFE OF A HOOD STAR
By **Ca$h & Rashia Wilson**

NIGHTMARES OF A HUSTLA 1-3
BLOOD AND GAMES 1&2
By **King Dream**

GHOST MOB
By **Stilloan Robinson**

HARD AND RUTHLESS 1&2
MOB TOWN 251
THE BILLIONAIRE BENTLEYS 1-3
REAL G'S MOVE IN SILENCE
By **Von Diesel**

MOB TIES 1-7
SOUL OF A HUSTLER, HEART OF A KILLER 1-3
GORILLAZ IN THE TRENCHES
OOPS CRY TOO 1&2
THE DAUGHTER OF A CARTEL BOSS
By **SayNoMore**

BODYMORE MURDERLAND 1-3
THE BIRTH OF A GANGSTER 1-4
By **Delmont Player**

FOR THE LOVE OF A BOSS 1&2
By **C. D. Blue**

KILLA KOUNTY 1-5
TENDER
By **Khufu**

MOBBED UP 1-4
THE BRICK MAN 1-5
THE COCAINE PRINCESS 1-10
STEPPERS 1-3
SUPER GREMLIN 1-4
A GANGSTA'S SON
By **King Rio**

MONEY GAME 1&2
By **Smoove Dolla**

A GANGSTA'S KARMA 1-5
By **FLAME**

KING OF THE TRENCHES 1-3
By **GHOST & TRANAY ADAMS**

BAD BITCHES WIT GUNZ 1&2
PROBLEM SOLVED
By "Christopher Diesel" Hornezes

QUEEN OF THE ZOO 1&2
By **Black Migo**

GRIMEY WAYS 1-3
BETRAYAL OF A G
By **Ray Vinci**

XMAS WITH AN ATL SHOOTER
By **Ca$h & Destiny Skai**

KING KILLA 1&2
By **Vincent "Vitto" Holloway**

BETRAYAL OF A THUG 1&2
By **Fre$h**

COUNTDOWN OF A KILLA 1&2
SEX, MURDER AND GOD 1&2
GUNS DOWN, BOTTOMS UP 1&2
By Lo-Life

THE MURDER QUEENS 1-7
By **Michael Gallon**

FOR THE LOVE OF BLOOD 1-4
By **Jamel Mitchell**

HOOD CONSIGLIERE 3 | KEESE

HOOD CONSIGLIERE 1&2
NO TIME FOR ERROR
By **Keese**

PROTÉGÉ OF A LEGEND 1,2&3
LOVE IN THE TRENCHES 1&2
By **Corey Robinson**

THE PLUG'S RUTHLESS DAUGHTER 1&2
By **Tony Daniels**

BORN IN THE GRAVE 1-3
CRIME PAYS
By **Self Made Tay**

MOAN IN MY MOUTH
By **XTASY**

TORN BETWEEN A GANGSTER AND A GENTLEMAN
By **J-BLUNT & Miss Kim**

LOYALTY IS EVERYTHING 1-3
CITY OF SMOKE 1-3
By **Molotti**

HERE TODAY GONE TOMORROW 1&2
By **Fly Rock**

WOMEN LIE MEN LIE 1-4
FIFTY SHADES OF SNOW 1-3
STACK BEFORE YOU SPLURGE
GIRLS FALL LIKE DOMINOES
NAÏVE TO THE STREETS
By **ROY MILLIGAN**

PILLOW PRINCESS
By **S. Hawkins**

HOOD CONSIGLIERE 3 | KEESE

THE BUTTERFLY MAFIA 1-3
SALUTE MY SAVAGERY 1&2
By **Fumiya Payne**

THE LANE 1&2
By Ken-Ken Spence

THE PUSSY TRAP 1-5
By **Nene Capri**

DIRTY DNA
By **Blaque**

SANCTIFIED AND HORNY
by **XTASY**

BOOKS BY LDP'S CEO, CA$H

TRUST IN NO MAN
TRUST IN NO MAN 2
TRUST IN NO MAN 3
BONDED BY BLOOD
SHORTY GOT A THUG
THUGS CRY
THUGS CRY 2
THUGS CRY 3
TRUST NO BITCH
TRUST NO BITCH 2
TRUST NO BITCH 3
TIL MY CASKET DROPS
RESTRAINING ORDER
RESTRAINING ORDER 2
IN LOVE WITH A CONVICT
LIFE OF A HOOD STAR
XMAS WITH AN ATL SHOOTER